Marx Machiavelli Chesterton Emerson Joyce
Abbott Hardy Montaigne Cooper Austen
Defoe Melville Haggard Hugo
Carroll Christie Eliot Grimm
Stoker Molière
Wilde Maupassant Byron
Engels Schiller
Garnett Einstein Fitzgerald Smith
Goethe Hawthorne Kafka
Cotton Dostoyevsky Hall
Baum Kipling Doyle Willis
Leslie Dumas Henry Nietzsche
Flaubert Turgenev Balzac
Stockton Vatsyayana Crane
Burroughs Whitman Verne
Curtis Tocqueville Gogol Vinci
Homer Widger Tolstoy Busch
Darwin Thoreau
Potter Freud Zola Twain Plato Scott
Lawrence
Kant Jowett Stevenson Dickens
Andersen Burton Hesse Harte
London Descartes Cervantes
Poe Aristotle Wells Voltaire
Hale James Hastings
Bunner Shakespeare Cooke
Richter Chambers Irving
da Benedict
Doré Swift Dante Chekhov Shaw Wodehouse Alcott
Pushkin
Newton

tredition®

tredition was established in 2006 by Sandra Latusseck and Soenke Schulz. Based in Hamburg, Germany, tredition offers publishing solutions to authors and publishing houses, combined with worldwide distribution of printed and digital book content. tredition is uniquely positioned to enable authors and publishing houses to create books on their own terms and without conventional manufacturing risks.

For more information please visit: www.tredition.com

## TREDITION CLASSICS

This book is part of the TREDITION CLASSICS series. The creators of this series are united by passion for literature and driven by the intention of making all public domain books available in printed format again - worldwide. Most TREDITION CLASSICS titles have been out of print and off the bookstore shelves for decades. At tredition we believe that a great book never goes out of style and that its value is eternal. Several mostly non-profit literature projects provide content to tredition. To support their good work, tredition donates a portion of the proceeds from each sold copy. As a reader of a TREDITION CLASSICS book, you support our mission to save many of the amazing works of world literature from oblivion. See all available books at www.tredition.com.

## Project Gutenberg

The content for this book has been graciously provided by Project Gutenberg. Project Gutenberg is a non-profit organization founded by Michael Hart in 1971 at the University of Illinois. The mission of Project Gutenberg is simple: To encourage the creation and distribution of eBooks. Project Gutenberg is the first and largest collection of public domain eBooks.

# The Story of a New York House

H. C. (Henry Cuyler) Bunner

# Imprint

This book is part of TREDITION CLASSICS

Author: H. C. (Henry Cuyler) Bunner
Cover design: Buchgut, Berlin – Germany

Publisher: tredition GmbH, Hamburg - Germany
ISBN: 978-3-8472-1510-3

www.tredition.com
www.tredition.de

THE STORY OF A NEW-YORK HOUSE
BY
H.C.BUNNER

Then out of the door came Jacob Dolph.

# THE STORY
# OF
# A NEW YORK HOUSE

BY

H. C. BUNNER

*ILLUSTRATED BY A. B. FROST*

NEW YORK
CHARLES SCRIBNER'S SONS
1887


Press of J. J. Little & Co.
Astor Place, New York.

TO

A. L. B.

LIST OF ILLUSTRATIONS.

[TOC] [1]

# THE STORY OF A NEW YORK HOUSE.

## I.

"I hear," said Mrs. Abram Van Riper, seated at her breakfast-table, and watching the morning sunlight dance on the front of the great Burrell house on the opposite side of Pine Street, "that the Dolphs are going to build a prodigious fine house out of town—somewhere up near the Rynders's place."

"And I hear," said Abram Van Riper, laying down last night's *Evening Post*, "that Jacob Dolph is going to give up business. And if he does, it's a disgrace to the town."

It was in the summer of 1807, and Abram Van Riper was getting well over what he considered the meridian line of sixty years. He was hale and hearty; his business was flourishing; his boy was turning out all that should [2] have been expected of one of the Van Riper stock; the refracted sunlight from the walls of the stately house occupied by the Cashier of the Bank of the United States lit with a subdued secondary glimmer the Van Riper silver on the breakfast-table—the squat teapot and slop-bowl, the milk-pitcher, that held a quart, and the apostle-spoon in the broken loaf-sugar on the Delft plate. Abram Van Riper was decorously happy, as a New York merchant should be. In all other respects, he was pleased to think, he was what a New York merchant should be, and the word of the law and the prophets was fulfilled with him and in his house.

"I'm sure," Mrs. Van Riper began again, somewhat querulously, "I can't see why Jacob Dolph shouldn't give up business, if he's so minded. He's a monstrous fortune, from all I hear—a good hundred thousand dollars."

"A hundred thousand dollars!" repeated her husband, scornfully. "Ay, and twice twenty thousand pounds on the top of that. He's done well, has Dolph. All the more reason he should stick to his trade; and not go to lolling [3] in the sun, like a runner at the Custom-House door. He's not within ten years of me, and here he must build his country house, and set up for the fine gentleman. Jacob

Dolph! Did I go on his note, when he came back from France, brave as my master, in '94, or did I not? And where 'ud he have raised twenty thousand in this town, if I hadn't? What's got into folks nowadays? Damn me if I can see!"

His wife protested, in wifely fashion. "I'm sure, Van Riper," she began, "you've no need to fly in such a huff if I so much as speak of folks who have some conceit of being genteel. It's only proper pride of Mr. Dolph to have a country house, and—"(her voice faltering a little, timorously) "ride in and—and out— —"

"*Ride!*" snorted Mr. Van Riper. "In a carriage, maybe?"

"In a carriage, Van Riper. You may think to ride in a carriage is like being the Pope of Rome; but there's some that knows better. And if you'd set up your carriage," went on the undaunted Mrs. Van Riper, "and gone over to Greenwich Street two years ago, as I'd [4] have had you, and made yourself friendly with those people there, I'd have been on the Orphan Asylum Board at this very minute; and *you* would— —"

Mr. Van Riper knew all that speech by heart, in all its variations. He knew perfectly well what it would end in, this time, although he was not a man of quick perception: "He would have been a member of the new Historical Society."

"Yes," he thought to himself, as he found his hat and shuffled out into Pine Street; "and John Pintard would have had my good check in his pocket for his tuppenny society. Pine Street is fine enough for me."

Mr. Van Riper had more cause for his petulancy than he would have acknowledged even to himself. He was a man who had kept his shop open all through Clinton's occupancy, and who had had no trouble with the British. And when they were gone he had had to do enough to clear his skirts of any smirch of Toryism, and to implant in his own breast a settled feeling of militant Americanism. He did not like it that the order of things [5] should change—and the order of things was changing. The town was growing out of all knowledge of itself. Here they had their Orphan Asylum, and their Botanical Garden, and their Historical Society; and the Jews were having it all their own way; and now people were talking of free schools, and of laying out a map for the upper end of the town to grow on, in the "system" of straight streets and avenues. To the devil with systems and avenues! said he. That was all the doing of those cursed Frenchmen. He knew how it would be when they brought their plaguy frigate here in the first fever year—'93—and the fools marched up from Peck's Slip after a red nightcap, and howled their cut-throat song all night long.

It began to hum itself in his head as he walked toward Water Street—*Ça ira—ça ira—les aristocrats à la lanterne.* A whiff of the wind that blew through Paris streets in the terrible times had come across the Atlantic and tickled his dull old Dutch nostrils.

But something worse than this vexed the conservative spirit of Abram Van Riper. He [6] could forgive John Pintard—whose inspiration, I think, foreran the twentieth century—his fancy for free schools and historical societies, as he had forgiven him his sidewalk-building fifteen years before; he could proudly overlook the fact that the women were busying themselves with all manner of wild charities; he could be contented though he knew that the Hebrew Hart was president of that merchants' club at Baker's, of which he himself would fain have been a member. But there was some thing in the air that he could neither forgive nor overlook, nor be contented with.

There was a change coming over the town—a change which he could not clearly define, even in his own mind. There was a great keeping of carriages, he knew. A dozen men had bought carriages, or were likely to buy them at any time. The women were forming societies for the improvement of this and that. And he, who had moved up-town from Dock Street, was now in an old-fashioned quarter. All this he knew, but the something which made him uneasy was more subtile.

Within the last few years he had observed [7] an introduction of certain strange distinctions in the social code of the town. It had been vaguely intimated to him—perhaps by his wife, he could not remember—that there was a difference between his trade and Jacob Dolph's trade. He was a ship-chandler. Jacob Dolph sold timber. Their shops were side by side; Jacob Dolph's rafts lay in the river in front of Abram Van Riper's shop, and Abram Van Riper had gone on Jacob Dolph's note, only a few years ago. Yet, it seemed that it was *genteel* of Jacob Dolph to sell timber, and it was not genteel of Abram Van Riper to be a ship-chandler. There was, then, a difference between Jacob Dolph and Abram Van Riper—a difference which, in forty years, Abram Van Riper had never conceived of. There were folks who held thus. For himself, he did not understand it. What difference there was between selling the wood to make a ship, and selling the stores to go inside of her, he could not understand.

The town was changing for the worse; he saw that. He did not wish—God forbid!—that his son John should go running about to [8] pleasure-gardens. But it would be no more than neighborly if these young bucks who went out every night should ask him to go with them. Were William Irving's boys and Harry Brevoort and those young Kembles too fine to be friends with his boy? Not that he'd go with them a-rollicking—no, not that—but 'twould be neighborly. It was all wrong, he thought; they were going whither they knew not, and wherefore they knew not; and with that he cursed their airs and their graces, and pounded down to the Tontine, to put his name at the head of the list of those who subscribed for a testimonial service of plate, to be presented to our esteemed fellow-citizen and valued associate, Jacob Dolph, on his retirement from active business.

Jacob Dolph at this moment was setting forth from his house in State Street, whose pillared balcony, rising from the second floor to the roof, caught a side glance of the morning sun, that loved the Battery far better than Pine Street. He had his little boy by the hand [9] —young Jacob, his miniature, his heir, and the last and only living one of his eight children. Mr. Dolph walked with his stock thrust out and the lower end of his waistcoat drawn in—he was Colonel Dolph, if he had cared to keep the title; and had come back from Monmouth with a hole in his hip that gave him a bit of a limp, even now in eighteen-hundred-and-seven. He and the boy marched forth like an army with a small but enthusiastic left wing, into the poplar-studded Battery. The wind blew fresh off the bay; the waves beat up against the seawall, and swirled with a chuckle under Castle Garden bridge. A large brig was coming up before the wind, all her sails set, as though she were afraid—and she was—of British frigates outside the Hook. Two or three fat little boats, cat-rigged, after the good old New York fashion, were beating down toward Staten Island, to hunt for the earliest blue-fish.

The two Dolphs crossed the Battery, where the elder bowed to his friends among the merchants who lounged about the city's pleasure-ground, lazily chatting over their business affairs. Then they turned up past Bowling [10] Green into Broadway, where Mr. Dolph kept on bowing, for half the town was out, taking the fresh morning for marketing and all manner of shopping. Everybody knew Jacob Dolph afar off by his blue coat with the silver buttons, his nankeen waistcoat, and his red-checked Indian silk neckcloth. He made it a sort of uniform. Captain Beare had brought him a bolt of nankeen and a silk kerchief every year since 1793, when Mr. Dolph gave him credit for the timber of which the *Ursa Minor* was built.

And everybody seemed willing to make acquaintance with young Jacob's London-made kerseymere breeches, of a bright canary color, and with his lavender silk coat, and with his little *chapeau de Paris*. Indeed, young Jacob was quite the most prominent moving spectacle on Broadway, until they came to John Street, and saw something rolling down the street that quite cut the yellow kerseymeres out of all popular attention.

This was a carriage, the body of which was shaped like a huge section of a cheese, set up on its small end upon broad, swinging straps [11] between two pairs of wheels. It was not unlike a piece of cheese in color, for it was of a dull and faded grayish-green, like mould, relieved by pale-yellow panels and gilt ornaments. It was truly an interesting structure, and it attracted nearly as much notice on Broadway in 1807 as it might to day. But it was received with far more reverence, for it was a court coach, and it belonged to the Des Anges family, the rich Huguenots of New Rochelle. It had been built in France, thirty years before, and had been sent over as a present to his brother from the Count des Anges, who had himself neglected to make use of his opportunities to embrace the Protestant religion.

When the white-haired old lady who sat in this coach, with a very little girl by her side, saw Mr. Dolph and his son, she leaned out of the window and signalled to the old periwigged driver to stop, and he drew up close to the sidewalk. And then Mr. Dolph and his son came up to the window and took off their hats, and made a great low bow and a small low bow to the old lady and the little girl. [12]

"Madam Des Anges," said Mr. Dolph, with an idiom which he had learned when he was presented at the court of Louis the Sixteenth, "has surely not driven down from New Rochelle this morning? That would tax even her powers."

Madam Des Anges did not smile—she had no taste for smiling—but she bridled amiably.

"No, Mr. Dolph," she replied; "I have been staying with my daughter-in-law, at her house at King's Bridge, and I have come to town to put my little granddaughter to school. She is to have the privilege of being a pupil of Mme. Dumesnil."

Madam Des Anges indicated the little girl with a slight movement, as though she did not wish to allow the child more consideration than a child deserved. The little girl turned a great pair of awed eyes, first on her grandmother, and then on the gentlemen, and spoke no word. Young Jacob Dolph stared hard at her, and then contemplated his kerseymeres with lazy satisfaction. He had no time for girls. And a boy who had his breeches made in London was a boy of consequence, and [13] need not concern himself about every one he saw.

"And this is your son, I make no doubt," went on Madam Des Anges; "you must bring him to see us at King's Bridge, while we are so near you. These young people should know each other."

Mr. Dolph said he would, and showed a becoming sense of the honor of the invitation; and he made young Jacob say a little speech of thanks, which he did with a doubtful grace; and then Mr. Dolph sent his compliments to Madam Des Anges' daughter-in-law, and Madam Des Anges sent her compliments to Mrs. Dolph, and there was more stately bowing, and the carriage lumbered on, with the little girl looking timorously out of the window, her great eyes fixed on the yellow kerseymeres, as they twinkled up the street.

"Papa," said young Jacob, as they turned the corner of Ann Street, "when may I go to a boys' school? I'm monstrous big to be at Mrs. Kilmaster's. And I don't like to be a girl-boy."

"Are you a girl-boy?" inquired his father, smiling. [14]

"Aleck Cameron called me one yesterday. He said I was a girl-boy because I went to dame-school. He called me Missy, too!" the boy went on, with his breast swelling.

"We'll see about it," said Mr. Dolph, smiling again; and they walked on in silence to Mrs. Kilmaster's door, where he struck the knocker, and a neat mulatto girl opened the narrow door. Then he patted his boy on the [15] head and bade him good-by for the morning, and told him to be a good boy at school. He took a step or two and looked back. Young Jacob lingered on the step, as if he had a further communication to make. He paused.

"I thumped him," said young Jacob, and the narrow door swallowed him up.

Mr. Dolph continued on his walk up Broadway. As he passed the upper end of the Common he looked with interest at the piles of red sandstone among the piles of white marble, where they were building the new City Hall. The Council had ordered that the rear or northward end of the edifice should be constructed of red stone; because red stone was cheap, and none but a few suburbans would ever look down on it from above Chambers Street. Mr. Dolph shook his head. He thought he knew better. He had watched the growth of trade; he knew the room for further growth; he had noticed the long converging lines of river-front, with their unbounded accommodation for wharves and slips. He believed that the day would come—and his own boy might see it—when the [16] business of the city would crowd the dwelling-houses from the river side, east and west, as far, maybe, as Chambers Street. He had no doubt that the boy might find himself, forty years from then, in a populous and genteel neighborhood. Perhaps he foresaw too much; but he had a jealous yearning for a house that should be a home for him, and for his child, and for his grandchildren. He wanted a place where his wife might have a garden; a place which the boy would grow up to love and cherish, where the boy might bring a wife some day. And even if it were a little out of town—why, his wife did not want a rout every night; and it was likely his old friends would come out and see him once in a while, and smoke a pipe in his garden and eat a dish of strawberries, perhaps.

As he thought it all over for the hundredth time, weighing for and against in his gentle and deliberative mind, he strolled far out of town. There was a house here and there on the road—a house with a trim, stiff little garden, full of pink and white and blue flowers in orderly, clam-shell-bordered beds. But it was [17] certainly, he had to admit, as he looked about him, very *countrified* indeed. It seemed that the city must lose itself if it wandered up here among these rolling meadows and wooded hills. Yet even up here, half way to Greenwich Village, there were little outposts of the town—clumps of neighborly houses, mostly of the poorer class, huddling together to form small nuclei for sporadic growth. There was one on his right, near the head of Collect Street. Perhaps that quizzical little old German was right, who had told him that King's Bridge property was a rational investment.

He went across the hill where Grand Street crosses Broadway, and up past what was then North and is to-day Houston Street, and then turned down a straggling road that ran east and west. He walked toward the Hudson, and passed a farmhouse or two, and came to a bare place where there were no trees, and only a few tangled bushes and ground-vines.

Here a man was sitting on a stone, awaiting him. As he came near, the man arose.

"Ah, it's you, Weeks? And have you the plan?" [18]

"Yes, Colonel—Mr. Dolph. I've put the window where you want it—that is, my brother Levi did—though I don't see as you're going to have much trouble in looking over anything that's likely to come between you and the river."

Mr. Dolph took the crisp roll of parchment [19] and studied it with loving interest. It had gone back to Ezra Weeks, the builder, and his brother Levi, the architect, for the twentieth time, perhaps. Was there ever an architect's plan put in the hands of a happy nest-builder where the windows did not go up and down from day to day, and the doors did not crawl all around the house, and the veranda did not contract and expand like a sensitive plant; or where the rooms and closets and corridors did not march backward and forward and in and out at the bidding of every fond, untutored whim?

"It's a monstrous great big place for a country-house, Mr. Dolph," said Ezra Weeks, as he looked over Jacob Dolph's shoulder at the drawings of the house, and shook his head with a sort of pitying admiration for the projector's audacity.

They talked for a while, and looked at the site as if they might see more in it than they saw yesterday, and then Weeks set off for the city, pledged to hire laborers and to begin the work on the morrow.

"I think I can get you some of that stone [20] that's going into the back of the City Hall, if you say so, Mr. Dolph. That stone was bought cheap, you know—bought for the city."

"See what you can do, Weeks," said Mr. Dolph; and Mr. Weeks went whistling down the road.

Jacob Dolph walked around his prospective domain. He kicked a wild blackberry bush aside, to look at the head of a stake, and tried to realize that that would be the corner of his house. He went to where the parlor fireplace would be, and stared at the grass and stones, wondering what it would be like to watch the fire flickering on the new hearth. Then he looked over toward the Hudson, and saw the green woods on Union Hill and the top of a white sail over the high river-bank. He hoped that no one would build a large house between him and the river.

He lingered so long that the smoke of midday dinners was arising from Greenwich Village when he turned back toward town. When he reached the Commons on his homeward way he came across a knot of idlers who were wasting [21] the hour of the noontide meal in gaping at the unfinished municipal building.

They were admiringly critical. One man was vociferously enthusiastic.

"It's a marvellous fine building, say I, sir! Worthy of the classic shades of antiquity. If Europe can show a finer than that will be when she's done, then, in *my* opinion, sir, Europe is doing well."

"You admire the architecture, Mr. Huggins?" asked Mr. Dolph, coming up behind him. Mr. Huggins turned around, slightly disconcerted, and assumed an amiability of manner such as can only be a professional acquirement among us poor creatures of human nature.

"Ah, Mr. Dolph—Colonel, I should say! I have purposed to do myself the honor of presenting myself at your house this afternoon, Colonel Dolph, to inquire if you did not desire to have your peruke *frisée*. For I had taken the liberty of observing you in conversation with Madam Des Anges this morning, in her equipage, and it had occurred to me that possibly the madam might be a-staying with you."

"Madam Des Anges does not honor my [22] house this time, Huggins," returned Mr. Dolph, with an indulgent little laugh; "and my poor old peruke will do very well for to-day."

There was a perceptible diminution in Mr. Huggins's ardor; but he was still suave.

"I hope the madam is in good health," he remarked.

"She is, I believe," said Mr. Dolph.

"And your good lady, sir? I have not had the pleasure of treating Mrs. Dolph professionally for some time, sir, I— —"

Mr. Dolph was wary. "I don't think Mrs. Dolph is fond of the latest modes, Huggins. But here comes Mr. Van Riper. Perhaps he will have his peruke *frisée*."

Mr. Huggins got out of a dancing-master's pose with intelligent alacrity, bade Mr. Dolph a hasty "Good-afternoon!" and hurried off toward his shop, one door above Wall Street. Mr. Van Riper did not like "John Richard Desbrosses Huggins, Knight of the Comb."

There was something else that Mr. Van Riper did not like.

"Hullo, Dolph!" he hailed his friend. "What's this I heard about you building a [23] preposterous tom-fool of a town-house out by Greenwich? Why don't you hire that house that Burr had, up near Lispenard's cow-pasture, and be done with it?"

Mr. Dolph seized his chance.

"It's not so preposterous as all that. By the way, talking of Burr, I hear from Richmond that he'll positively be tried next week. Did you know that young Irving—William's son, the youngest, the lad that writes squibs—has gone to Richmond for the defence?"

"William Irving's son might be in better business," grunted Mr. Van Riper, for a moment diverted. "If we'd got at that devil when he murdered poor Hamilton—'fore gad, we'd have saved the trouble of trying him. Do you remember when we was for going to Philadelphia after him, and there the sly scamp was at home all the time up in his fine house, a-sitting in a tub of water, reading French stuff, as cool as a cowcumber, with the whole town hunting for him?" Then he came back. "But that house of yours. You haven't got this crazy notion that New York's going to turn into London while you smoke [24] your pipe, have you? You're keeping some of your seven business senses, ain't you?"

"I don't know," Mr. Dolph mildly defended his hobby; "there is a great potentiality of growth in this city. Here's an estimate that John Pintard made the other day— —"

"John Pintard! He's another like *you*!" said Mr. Van Riper.

"Well, look at it for yourself," pleaded the believer in New York's future.

Mr. Van Riper took the neatly written paper, and simply snorted and gasped as he read this:

*Statistical.*

By the numeration of the inhabitants of this city, recently published, the progress of population for the last 5 years appears to be at the rate of 25 per cent. Should our city continue to increase in the same proportion during the present century, the aggregate number at its close will far exceed that of any other city in the Old World, Pekin not excepted, as will appear from the following table. Progress of population in the city of New York, computed at the rate of 25 per cent, every 5 years:

| | | | |
|---|---|---|---|
| 1805 | 75,770 | 1855 | 705,650 |
| 1810 | 95,715 | 1860 | 882,062 |
| 1815 | 110,390 | 1865 | 1,102,577 |
| 1820 | 147,987 | 1870 | 1,378,221 |
| 1825 | 184,923 | 1875 | 1,722,776 |
| 1830 | 231,228 | 1880 | 2,153,470 |

| | | | |
|---|---|---|---|
| 1835 | 289,035 | 1885 | 2,691,837 |
| 1840 | 361,293 | 1890 | 3,364,796 |
| 1845 | 451,616 | 1895 | 4,205,995 |
| 1850 | 564,520 | 1900 | 5,257,493 |

[25]

When he had read it through he was a-quivering, crimson with that rage of Conservative indignation which is even more fervent than the flames of Radical enthusiasm.

"Yes," he said; "there's seventy-five thousand people in this town, and there'll be seventy-five thousand bankrupts if this lunacy goes on. And there's seventy-five thousand maggots in your brain, and seventy-five thousand in John Pintard's; and if you two live to see nineteen hundred, you'll have twice five million two hundred and fifty-seven thousand four hundred and ninety-three—whatever that may be!" And he thrust the paper back at Jacob Dolph, and made for the Tontine and the society of sensible men.

The house was built, in spite of Abram Van Riper's remonstrance. It had a stone front, almost flush with the road, and brick gable-ends, in each one of which, high up near the roof, stood an arched window, to lift an eyebrow to the sun, morning and evening. But it was only a country-house, after all; and the [26] Dolphs set up their carriage and drove out and in, from June to September.

There was a garden at the side, where Mrs. Dolph could have the flowers her heart had yearned after ever since Jacob Dolph brought her from her home at Rondout, when she was seventeen.

Strengthened by the country air—so they said—young Jacob grew clean out of his dame-school days and into and out of Columbia College, and was sent abroad, a sturdy youth, to have a year's holiday. It was to the new house that he came back the next summer, with a wonderful stock of fine clothes and of finer manners, and with a pair of mustaches that scandalized everybody but Madam Des Anges, who had seen the like in France when she visited her brother. And a very fine young buck was young Jacob, altogether, with his knowledge of French and his ignorance of Dutch, and a way he had with the women, and another way he had with the men, and his heirship to old Jacob Dolph's money and his two houses. [27]

For they stayed in the old house until 1822.

It was a close, hot night in the early summer; there was a thick, warm mist that turned now and then into a soft rain; yet every window in the Dolphs' house on State Street was closed.

It had been a hideous day for New York. From early morning until long after dark had set in, the streets had been filled with frightened, disordered crowds. The city was again stricken with the old, inevitable, ever-recurring scourge of yellow fever, and the people had lost their heads. In every house, in every office and shop, there was hasty packing, mad confusion, and wild flight. It was only a question of getting out of town as best one might. Wagons and carts creaked and rumbled and rattled through every street, piled high with household chattels, up-heaped in blind haste. Women rode on the swaying loads, or walked beside with the smaller children in their arms. Men bore heavy burdens, and children helped according to their strength. There was only [28] one idea, and that was flight—from a pestilence whose coming might have been prevented, and whose course could have been stayed. To most of these poor creatures the only haven seemed to be Greenwich Village; but some sought the scattered settlements above; some crossed to Hoboken; some to Bushwick; while others made a long journey to Staten Island, across the bay. And when they reached their goals, it was to beg or buy lodgings anywhere and anyhow; to sleep in cellars and garrets, in barns and stables.

The panic was not only among the poor and ignorant. Merchants were moving their offices, and even the Post Office and the Custom [29] House were to be transferred to Greenwich. There were some who remained faithful throughout all, and who labored for the stricken, and whose names are not even written in the memory of their fellow-men. But the city had been so often ravaged before, that at the first sight there was one mere animal impulse of flight that seized upon all alike.

At one o'clock, when some of the better streets had once more taken on their natural quiet, an ox-cart stood before the door of the Dolphs' old house. A little behind it stood the family carriage, its lamps unlit. The horses stirred uneasily, but the oxen waited in dull, indifferent patience. Presently the door opened, and two men came out and awkwardly bore a plain coffin to the cart. Then they mounted to the front of the cart, hiding between them a muffled lantern. They wore cloths over the lower part of their faces, and felt hats drawn low over their eyes. Something in their gait showed them to be seafaring men, or the like.

Then out of the open door came Jacob Dolph, moving with a feeble shuffle between [30] his son and his old negro coachman—this man and his wife the only faithful of all the servants. The young man put his father in the carriage, and the negro went back and locked the doors and brought the keys to his young master. He mounted to the box, and through the darkness could be seen a white towel tied around his arm—the old badge of servitude's mourning.

The oxen were started up, and the two vehicles moved up into Broadway. They travelled with painful slowness; the horses had to be held in to keep them behind the cart, for the oxen could be only guided by the whip, and not by word of mouth. The old man moaned a little at the pace, and quivered when he heard the distant sound of hammers.

"What is it?" he asked, nervously.

"They are boarding up some of the streets," said his son; "do not fear, father. Everything is prepared; and if we make no noise, we shall not be troubled."

"If we can only keep her out of the Potter's Field—the Potter's Field!" cried the father; "I'll thank God—I'll ask no more—I'll ask no more!" [31]

And then he broke down and cried a little, feebly, and got his son's hand in the darkness and put on his own shoulder.

It was nearly two when they came to St. Paul's and turned the corner to the gate. It was dark below, but some frenzied fools were burning tar-barrels far down Ann Street, and the light flickered on the top of the church spire. They crossed the churchyard to where a shallow grave had been dug, half way down the hill. The men lowered the body into it; the old negro gave them a little *rouleau* of coin, and they went hurriedly away into the night.

The clergyman came out by and by, with the sexton behind him. He stood high up above the grave, and drew his long cloak about him and lifted an old pomander-box to his face. He was not more foolish than his fellows; in that evil hour men took to charms and to saying of spells. Below the grave and apart, for the curse rested upon them, too, stood Jacob Dolph and his son, the old man leaning on the arm of the younger. Then the clergyman began to read the service for the burial of the [32] dead, over the departed sister—and wife and mother. He spoke low; but his voice seemed [33] to echo in the stillness. He came forward with a certain shrinking, and cast the handful of dust and ashes into the grave. When it was done, the sexton stepped forward and rapidly threw in the earth until he had filled the little hollow even with the ground. Then, with fearful precaution, he laid down the carefully cut sods, and smoothed them until there was no sign of what had been done. The clergyman turned to the two mourners, without moving nearer to them, and lifted up his hands. The old man tried to kneel; but his son held him up, for he was too feeble, and they bent their heads for a moment of silence. The clergyman went away as he had come; and Jacob Dolph and his son went back to the carriage. When his father was seated, young Jacob Dolph said to the coachman: "To the new house."

The heavy coach swung into Broadway, and climbed up the hill out into the open country. There were lights still burning in the farmhouses, bright gleams to east and west, but the silence of the damp summer night hung over the sparse suburbs, and the darkness [34] seemed to grow more intense as they drove away from the city. The trees by the roadside were almost black in the gray mist; the raw, moist smell of the night, the damp air, chilly upon the high land, came in through the carriage windows. Young Jacob looked out and noted their progress by familiar landmarks on the road; but the old man sat with his head bent on his new black stock.

It was almost three, and the east was beginning to look dark, as though a storm were settling there in the grayness, when they turned down the straggling street and drew up before the great dark mass that was the new house. The carriage-wheels gritted against the loose stones at the edge of the roadway, and the great door of the house swung open. The light of one wavering candle-flame, held high above her head, fell on the black face of old Chloe, the coachman's wife. There were no candles burning on the high-pitched stairway; all was dark behind her in the empty house.

Young Jacob Dolph helped his father to the ground, and between the young man and the negro old Jacob Dolph wearily climbed the [35] steps. Chloe lifted her apron to her face, and turned to lead them up the stair. Her husband went out to his horses, shutting the door softly after him, between Jacob Dolph's old life and the new life that was to begin in the new house.

[TOC] [36]

## II.

When young Jacob Dolph came down to breakfast the next morning he found his father waiting for him in the breakfast-room. The meal was upon the table. Old Chloe stood with her black hands folded upon her white apron, and her pathetic negro eyes following the old gentleman as he moved wistfully about the room.

Father and son shook hands in silence, and turned to the table. There were three chairs in their accustomed places. They hesitated a half-second, looking at the third great arm-chair, as though they waited for the mistress of the house to take her place. Then they sat down. It was six years before any one took that third chair, but every morning Jacob Dolph the elder made that little pause before he put himself at the foot of the table.

On this first morning there was very little said and very little eaten. But when they had made an end of sitting at the table old [37] Jacob Dolph said, with something almost like testiness in his husky voice:

"Jacob, I want to sell the house."

"Father!"

"The old house, I mean; I shall never go back there."

His son looked at him with a further inquiry. He felt a sudden new apprehension. The father sat back in his easy-chair, drumming on the arms with nervous fingers. [38]

"I shall never go back there," he said again.

"Of course you know best, sir," said young Jacob, gently; "but would it be well to be precipitate? It is possible that you may feel differently some time— —"

"There is no 'some time' for me!" broke in the old man, gripping the chair-arms, fiercely; "my time's done—done, sir!"

Then his voice broke and became plaintively kind.

"There, there! Forgive me, Jacob, boy. But it's true, my boy, true. The world's done, for me; but there's a world ahead for you, my son, thank God! I'll be patient—I'll be patient. God has been good to me, and I haven't many years to wait, in the course of nature."

He looked vacantly out of the window, trying to see the unforeseen with his mental sight.

"While I'm here, Jacob, let the old man have his way. It's a whimsey; I doubt 'tis hardly rational. But I have no heart to go home. Let me learn to live my life here. 'Twill be easier." [39]

"But do you think it necessary to sell, sir? Could you not hold the house? Are you certain that you would like to have a stranger living there?"

"I care not a pin who lives within those four walls now, sir!" cried the elder, with a momentary return of his vehemence. "It's no house to me now. Sell it, sir, sell it!—if there's any one will give money for it at a time like this. Bring every stick of furniture and every stitch of carpet up here; and let me have my way, Jacob—it won't be for long."

He got up and went blindly out of the room, and his son heard him muttering, "Not for long—not for long, now," as he wandered about the house and went aimlessly into room after room.

Old Jacob Dolph had always been an indulgent parent, and none kinder ever lived. But we should hardly call him indulgent to-day. Good as he was to his boy, it had always been with the goodness of a superior. It was the way of his time. A half-century ago the child's position was equivocal. He lived by the grace of God and his parents, and their [40] duty to him was rather a duty to society, born of an abstract morality. Love was given him, not as a right, but as an indulgence. And young Jacob Dolph, in all his grief and anxiety, was guiltily conscious of a secret thrill of pleasure—natural enough, poor boy!—in his sudden elevation to the full dignity of manhood, and his father's abdication of the headship of the house.

A little later in the day, urged again by the old gentleman, he put on his hat and went to see Abram Van Riper. Mr. Van Riper was now, despite his objections to the pernicious institution of country-houses, a near neighbor of the Dolphs. He had yielded, not to fashion, but to yellow fever, and at the very first of the outbreak had bought a house on the outskirts of Greenwich Village, and had moved there in unseemly haste. He had also registered an unnecessarily profane oath that he would never again live within the city limits.

When young Jacob Dolph came in front of the low, hip-roofed house, whose lower story of undressed stone shone with fresh whitewash, Mr. Van Riper stood on his stoop and [41] checked his guest at the front gate, a dozen yards away. From this distance he jabbed his big gold-headed cane toward the young man, as though to keep him off.

"Stay there, sir—you, sir, you Jacob Dolph!" he roared, brandishing the big stick. "Stand back, I tell you! Don't come in, sir! Good-day, sir—good-day, good-day, good- [42] day!" (This hurried excursus was in deference to a sense of social duty.) "Keep away, confound you, keep away—consume your body, sir, stay where you are!"

"I'm not coming any nearer, Mr. Van Riper," said Jacob Dolph, with a smile which he could not help.

"I can't have you in here, sir," went on Mr. Van Riper, with no abatement of his agitation. "I don't want to be inhospitable; but I've got a wife and a son, sir, and you're infectious—damn it, sir, you're infectious!"

"I'll stay where I am, Mr. Van Riper," said young Jacob, smiling again. "I only came with a message from my father."

"With a what?" screamed Mr. Van Riper. "I can't have—oh, ay, a message! Well, say it then and be off, like a sensible youngster. Consume it, man, can't you talk farther out in the street?"

When Mr. Van Riper learned his visitor's message, he flung his stick on the white pebbles of the clam-shell-bordered path, and swore that he, Van Riper, was the only sane man in a city of lunatics, and that if Jacob Dolph tried [43] to carry out his plan he should be shipped straightway to Bloomingdale.

But young Jacob had something of his father's patience, and, despite the publicity of the interview, he contrived to make Mr. Van Riper understand how matters stood. To tell the truth, Van Riper grew quite sober and manageable when he realized that his extravagant imputation of insanity was not so wide of the mark as it might have seemed, and that there was a possibility that his old friend's mind might be growing weak. He even ventured a little way down the path and permitted Jacob to come to the gate while they discussed the situation.

"Poor old Dolph—poor old Jacob!" he groaned. "We must keep him out of the hands of the sharks, that we must!" He did not see young Jacob's irrepressible smile at this singular extension of metaphor. "He mustn't be allowed to sell that house in open market—never, sir! Confound it, I'll buy it myself before I'll see him fleeced!"

In the end he agreed, on certain strict conditions of precaution, to see young Jacob the [44] next day and discuss ways and means to save the property.

"Come here, sir, at ten, and I'll see you in the sitting-room, and we'll find out what we can do for your father—curse it, it makes me feel bad; by gad, it does! Ten to-morrow, then—and come fumigated, young man, don't you forget that—come fumigated, sir!"

It was Van Riper who bought the property at last. He paid eighteen thousand dollars for it. This was much less than its value; but it was more than any one else would have given just at that time, and it was all that Van Riper could afford. The transaction weighed on the purchaser's mind, however. He had bought the house solely out of kindness, at some momentary inconvenience to himself; and yet it looked as though he were taking advantage of his friend's weakness. Abram Van Riper was a man who cultivated a clear conscience, of a plain, old-fashioned sort, and the necessity for self-examination was novel and disagreeable to him.

Life lived itself out at Jacob Dolph's new [45] house whether he liked it or not. The furniture came up-town, and was somewhat awkwardly disposed about its new quarters; and in this unhomelike combination of two homes old Mr. Dolph sat himself down to finish his stint of life. He awoke each morning and found that twenty-four hours of sleep and waking lay before him, to be got through in their regular order, just as they were lived through by men who had an interest in living. He went to bed every night, and crossed off one from a tale of days of which he could not know the length.

Of course his son, in some measure, saved his existence from emptiness. He was proud of young Jacob—fond and proud. He looked upon him as a prince of men, which he was, indeed. He trusted absolutely in the young man, and his trust was well placed. And he knew that his boy loved him. But he had an old man's sad consciousness that he was not necessary to Jacob—that he was an adjunct, at the best, not an integral part of this younger existence. He saw Jacob the younger gradually recovering from his grief for the mother who [46] had left them; and he knew that even so would Jacob some day recover from grief when his father should have gone.

He saw this; but it is doubtful if he felt it acutely. Nature was gradually dulling his sensibilities with that wonderful anæsthetic of hers, which is so much kinder to the patient than it is to his watching friends. After the first wild freak of selling the house, he showed, for a long time, no marked signs of mental impairment, beyond his lack of interest in the things which he had once cared about—even in the growth of the city he loved. And in a lonely and unoccupied man, sixty-five years of age, this was not unnatural. It was not unnatural, even, if now and then he was whimsical, and took odd fancies and prejudices. But nevertheless the work was going on within his brain, little by little, day by day.

He settled his life into an almost mechanical routine, of which the most active part was his daily walk down into the city. At first he would not go beyond St. Paul's churchyard; but after awhile he began to take timorous strolls among the old business streets where [47] his life had been passed. He would drop into the offices of his old friends, and would read the market reports with a pretence of great interest, and then he would fold up his spectacles and put them in their worn leather case, and walk slowly out. He was always pleased when one of the younger clerks bowed to him and said, "Good-day, Mr. Dolph!"

It was in the fourth year of his widowhood that he bethought himself of young Jacob's need of a more liberal social life than he had been leading. The boy went about enough; [48] he was a good deal of a beau, so his father heard; and there was no desirable house in the town that did not welcome handsome, amiable young Dolph. But he showed no signs of taking a wife unto himself, and in those days the bachelor had only a provisional status in society. He was expected to wed, and the whole circle of his friends chorused yearly a deeper regret for the lost sheep, as time made that detestable thing, an "old bachelor," of him.

Young Jacob was receiving many courtesies and was making no adequate return. He felt it himself, but he was too tender of his father's changeless grief to urge him to open the great empty house to their friends. The father, however, felt that it was his duty to sacrifice his own desire for solitude, and, when the winter of 1825 brought home the city's wandering children—there were not so many of the wandering sort in 1825—he insisted that young Jacob should give a dinner to his friends among the gay young bachelors. That would be a beginning; and if all went well they would have an old maiden aunt from Philadelphia to [49] spend the winter with them, and help them to give the dinner parties which do not encourage bachelorhood, but rather convert and reform the coy celibate.

The news went rapidly through the town. The Dolph hospitality had been famous, and this was taken for a signal that the Dolph doors were to open again. There was great excitement in Hudson Street and St. John's Park. Maidens, bending over their tambour-frames, working secret hopes and aspirations in with their blossoming silks and worsted, blushed, with faint speculative smiles, as they thought of the vast social possibilities of the mistress of the grand Dolph house. Young bachelors, and old bachelors, too, rolled memories of the Dolph Madeira over longing tongues.

The Dolph cellar, too, had been famous, and just at that period New Yorkers had a fine and fanciful taste in wine, if they had any self-respect whatever.

I think it must have been about then that Mr. Dominick Lynch began his missionary labors among the smokers and drinkers of this

[50] city; he who bought a vineyard in France and the Vuelta Abajo plantations in Cuba, solely to teach the people of his beloved New York what was the positively proper thing in wines and cigars. If it was not then, it could not have been much later that Mr. Dolph had got accustomed to receiving, every now and then, an unordered and unexpected consignment of wines or Havana cigars, sent up from Little Dock Street—or what we call Water Street now, the lower end of it. And I am sure that he paid Mr. Lynch's bill with glowing pride; for Mr. Lynch extended the evangelizing hand of culture to none but those of pre-eminent social position.

It was to be quite a large dinner; but it was noticeable that none of the young men who were invited had engagements of regrettable priority.

Jacob Dolph the elder looked more interested in life than he had looked in four years when he stood on the hearthrug in the drawing-room and received his son's guests. He was a bold figure among all the young men, not only because he was tall and white-haired, [51] and for the moment erect, and of a noble and gracious cast of countenance, but because he clung to his old style of dress—his knee-breeches and silk stockings, and his long coat, black, for this great occasion, but of the "shadbelly" pattern. He wore his high black stock, too, and his snow-white hair was gathered behind into a loose peruke.

The young men wore trousers, or pantaloons, as they mostly called them, strapped under their varnished boots. Their coats were [52] cut like our dress-coats, if you can fancy them with a wild amplitude of collar and lapel. They wore large cravats and gaudy waistcoats, and two or three of them who had been too much in England came with shawls or rugs around their shoulders.

They were a fashionable lot of people, and this was a late dinner, so they sat down at six o'clock in the great dining-room—not the little breakfast-room—with old Jacob Dolph at one end of the table and young Jacob Dolph at the other.

It was a pleasant dinner, and the wine was good, and the company duly appreciative, although individually critical.

Old Jacob Dolph had on his right an agreeable French count, just arrived in New York, who was creating a *furor*; and on his left was Mr. Philip Waters, the oldest of the young men, who, being thirty-five, had a certain consideration for old age. But old Jacob Dolph was not quite at his ease. He did not understand the remarkable decorum of the young men. He himself belonged to the age of "bumpers and no heel taps," and nobody at [53] his board to-night seemed to care about drinking bumpers, even out of the poor, little, newfangled claret-glasses, that held only a thimbleful apiece. He had never known a lot of gentlemen, all by themselves, to be so discreet. Before the evening was over he became aware of the fact that he was the only man who was proposing toasts, and then he proposed them no more.

Things had changed since he was a young buck, and gave bachelor parties. Why, he could remember seeing his own good father—an irreproachable gentleman, surely—lock the door of his dining-room on the inside—ay, at just such a dinner as this—and swear that no guest of his should go out of that room sober. And his word had been kept. Times were changing. He thought, somehow, that these young men needed more good port in their veins.

Toward the end of the festivities he grew silent. He gave no more toasts, and drank no more bumpers, although he might safely have put another bottle or two under his broad waistcoat. But he leaned back in his chair, [54] and rested one hand on the table, playing with his wineglass in an absent-minded way. There was a vague smile on his face; but every now and then he knit his heavy gray brows as if he were trying to work out some problem of memory. Mr. Philip Waters and the French count were talking across him; he had been in the conversation, but he had dropped out some time before. At last he rose, with his brows knit, and pulled out his huge watch, and looked at its face. Everybody turned toward him, and, at the other end of the table, his son half rose to his feet. He put the watch back in his pocket, and said, in his clear, deep voice: "Gentlemen, I think we will rejoin the ladies."

There was a little impulsive stir around the table, and then he seemed to understand that he had wandered, and a frightened look came over his face. He tottered backward, and swayed from side to side. Mr. Philip Waters and the Frenchman had their arms behind him before he could fall, and in a second or two he had straightened himself up. He made a stately, tremulous apology for what he called [55] his "infelicitous absence of mind," and then he marched off to bed by himself, suffering no one to go with him.

And then he marched off to bed by himself, suffering no one to go with him.

A little while later in the evening, Mr. Philip Waters, walking down Broadway (which thoroughfare was getting to have a fairly suburban look), informed the French count that in his, Mr. Waters's, opinion, young Jacob Dolph would own that house before long.

Young Jacob Dolph's father insisted on repetitions of the bachelor dinner, but he never again appeared in the great dining-room. When there was a stag party he took his own simple dinner at five o'clock and went to bed early, and lay awake until his son had dismissed the last mild reveller, and he could hear the light, firm, young footstep mounting the stairs to the bedroom door opposite his own.

That was practically the end of it for old Jacob Dolph. The maiden aunt, who had been invited, was notified that she could not come, for Mr. Dolph was not well enough to open his house that winter.

But it was delicately [56] intimated to her that if he grew worse she might still be sent for, and that alleviated her natural disappointment. She liked to give parties; but there is also a chastened joy for some people in being at the head of a house of mourning.

Old Mr. Dolph grew no worse physically, except that he was inclined to make his daily walks shorter, and that he grew fonder of sitting at home in the little breakfast-room, where the sun shone almost all day long, and where Mrs. Dolph had once been fond of coming to sew. Her little square work-table of mahogany stood there still. There the old gentleman liked to dine, and often he dined alone. Young Jacob was in great demand all over town, and his father knew that he ought to go out and amuse himself. And the young man, although he was kind and loving, and never negligent in any office of respect or affection, had that strong youth in him which makes it impossible to sit every day of the week opposite an old man whose world had slipped by him, who knew nothing of youth except to love it and wonder at it. [57]

In the morning, before he went out for his daily tramp into town, old Jacob would say to young Jacob:

"I suppose I shall see you at dinner, my boy?"

And young Jacob would say, "Yes, sir," or "No, sir, I think not. Mrs. Des Anges was in town yesterday, and she asked me to ride up there to-day and dine. And Diana" (Diana was his big black mare) "needs a little work; she's getting badly out of condition. So, if it doesn't matter to you, sir, I'll just run up there and get back before the moon sets."

And the father would answer that it didn't matter, and would send his best respects, through Mrs. Des Anges at King's Bridge, to Madam Des Anges at New Rochelle; and at night he would sit down alone to his dinner in the breakfast-room, served by old Chloe, who did her humble best to tempt his appetite, which was likely to be feeble when Master Jacob was away.

Master Jacob had taken to riding to King's Bridge of late. Sometimes he would start out [58] early in the morning, just about the time when young Van Riper was plodding by on his way to the shop. Young Van Riper liked to be at the shop an hour earlier than his father. Old Mr. Dolph was always up, on these occasions, to see his son start off. He loved to look at the boy, in his English riding-boots and breeches, astride of black Diana, who pranced and curvetted up the unpaved road. Young Jacob had her well in hand, but he gave her her head and let her play until they reached Broadway, where he made her strike a rattling regular pace until they got well up the road; and then she might walk up Bloomingdale way or across to Hickory Lane.

If he went up by the east he was likely to dismount at a place which you can see now, a little west and south of McComb's Dam Bridge, where there is a bit of a rocky hollow, and a sort of horizontal cleft in the rocks that has been called a cave, and a water-washed stone above, whose oddly shaped depression is called an Indian's footprint. He would stop there, because right in that hollow, as I can [59] tell you myself, grew, in his time as in mine, the first of the spring flowers. It was full of violets once, carpeted fairly with the pale, delicate petals.

And up toward the west, on a bridle-path between the hills and the river, as you came toward Fort Washington, going to Tubby Hook—we are refined nowadays, and Tubby Hook is "Inwood"—Heaven help it!—there were wonderful flowers in the woods. The wind-flowers came there early, nestling under the gray rocks that sparkled with garnets; and there bloomed great bunches of Dutchman's-breeches—not the thin sprays that come in the late New England spring, but huge clumps that two men could not enclose with linked hands; great masses of scarlet and purple, and—mostly—of a waxy white, with something deathlike in their translucent beauty. There, also, he would wade into the swamps around a certain little creek, lured by a hope of the jack-in-the-pulpit, to find only the odorous and disappointing skunk-cabbage. And there the woods were full of the aroma of sassafras, and of birch tapped by the earliest woodpecker, [60] whose drumming throbbed through the young man's deep and tender musing.

And—strange enough for a young man who rides only to exercise his black mare—he never came out of those woods without an armful of columbine or the like. And—strange enough for any young man in this world of strange things—when he sat down at the table of Mrs. Des Anges, in her pleasant house near Harlem Creek, Miss Aline Des Anges wore a bunch of those columbines at her throat. Miss Aline Des Anges was a slim girl, not very tall, with great dark eyes that followed some people with a patient wistfulness.

One afternoon, in May of 1827, young Jacob found his father in the breakfast-room, and said to him:

"Father, I am going to marry Aline Des Anges."

His father, who had been dozing in the sun by the south window, raised his eyes to his son's face with a kindly, blank look, and said, thoughtfully:

"Des Anges. That's a good family, Jacob, [61] and a wonderful woman, Madam Des Anges. Is she alive yet?"

When Madam Des Anges, eighty years old, and strong and well, heard of this, she said:

"It is the etiquette of France that one family should make the proposition to the other family. Under the circumstances *I* will be the family that proposes. I will make a precedent. The Des Anges make precedents."

And she rode down to the Dolph house in the family carriage—the last time it ever went out—and made her "proposition" to Jacob Dolph the elder, and he brightened up most wonderfully, until you would have thought him quite his old self, and he told her what an honor he esteemed the alliance, and paid her compliments a hundred words long.

And in May of the next year, King's Bridge being out of the question, and etiquette being waived at the universal demand of society, the young couple stood up in the drawing-room of the Dolph house to be wed.

The ceremony was fashionably late—seven [62] o'clock in the evening. And after it was over, and the young couple had digested what St. Paul had to say about the ordinance of wedlock, and had inaudibly promised to do and be whatever the domine required of them, they were led by the half-dozen groomsmen to the long glass between the front windows, and made to stand up there, with their faces toward the company, and to receive the congratulations of a mighty procession of friends, who all used the same formulas, except the very old ones, who were delicately indelicate.

The bridegroom wore a blue coat and trousers, and a white satin waistcoat embroidered with silver-thread roses and lilies-of-the-valley. The coat was lined with cream-colored satin, quilted in a most elaborate pattern; and his necktie was of satin, too, with embroidered ends. His shirt was a miracle of fine linen. As to the bride, she was in white satin and lace, and at her throat she wore a little bunch of late white columbines, for which Mr. Jacob Dolph the younger had scoured the woods near Fort Washington.

There was to be a grand supper, later; and [63] the time of waiting was filled up with fashionable conversation.

That dear old doctor, who was then a dear young doctor, and whose fine snow-crowned face stood in later years as an outward and visible sign of all that was brave, kindly, self-sacrificing, and benevolent in the art of healing, was seated by Madam Des Anges, and was telling her, in stately phrase, suited to his auditor, of a certain case of heroism with which he had met in the course of his practice. Mr. Blank, it appeared, had been bitten by a dog that was supposed to be possessed by the rabies. For months he had suffered the agonies of mental suspense and of repeated cauterizing of the flesh, and during those months had concealed his case from his wife, that he might spare her pain—suffering in silence enough to unnerve most men.

"It was heroic," said Dr. F.

Madam Des Anges bowed her gray head approvingly.

"I think," she said, "his conduct shows him to be a man of taste. Had he informed his wife of his condition, she might have experienced [64] the most annoying solicitude; and I am informed that she is a person of feeble character."

The doctor looked at her, and then down at the floor; and then he asked her if she did not hope that Almaviva Lynch would bring Garcia back again, with that marvellous Italian opera, which, as he justly observed, captivated the eye, charmed the ear, and awakened the profoundest emotions of the heart.

And at that Madam Des Anges showed some animation, and responded that she had listened to some pleasing operas in Paris; but she did not know that they were of Italian origin.

But if Madam Des Anges was surprised to learn that any good thing could come out of any other country than France, there was another surprise in store for her, and it did not long impend.

It was only a little while after this that her grandson-in-law, finding her on his right and Abram Van Riper on his left—he had served out his time as a statue in front of the mirror—thought it proper to introduce to Madam [65] Des Anges his father's old friend, Mr. Van Riper. Mr. Van Riper bowed as low as his waistcoat would allow, and courteously observed that the honor then accorded him he had enjoyed earlier in the evening through the kind offices of Mr. Jacob Dolph, senior.

Madam Des Anges dandled her quizzing-glass as though she meant to put it up to her eye, and said, in a weary way:

"Mr.—ah—Van Riper must pardon me. I have not the power of remembering faces that some people appear to have; and my eyes—my eyes are not strong."

Old Van Riper stared at her, and he turned a turkey-cock purple all over his face, down to the double chin that hung over his white neckerchief.

"If your ladyship has to buy spectacles," he sputtered, "it needn't be on my account."

And he stamped off to the sideboard and tried to cool his red-hot rage with potations of Jamaica rum. There his wife found him. She had drawn near when she saw him talking with the great Madam Des Anges, and she had heard, as she stood hard by and smiled unobtrusively, [66] the end of that brief conversation. Her face, too, was flushed—a more fiery red than her flame-colored satin dress.

She attacked him in a vehement whisper.

"Van Riper, what are you doing? I'd almost believe you'd had too much liquor, if I didn't know you hadn't had a drop. Will you ever learn what gentility is? D'ye want us to live and die like toads in a hole? Here you are with your ill manners, offending Madam Des

Anges, that everybody knows is the best of the best, and there's an end of all likelihood of ever seeing her and her folks, and two nieces unmarried and as good girls as ever was, and such a connection for your son, who hasn't been out of the house it's now twelve months—except to this very wedding here, and you've no thought of your family when once you lose that mighty fine temper of yours, that you're so prodigious proud of; and where you'll end us, Van Riper, is more than I know, I vow."

But all she could get out of Van Riper was:

"The old harridan! She'll remember my name this year or two to come, I'll warrant ye!"

[67]

It was all over at last, and old black Julius, who had been acting as a combination of link-boy and major-domo at the foot of the front steps, extinguished his lantern, and went to bed, some time before a little white figure stole up the stairs and slipped into a door that Chloe—black Chloe—held open.

And the next day Jacob Dolph the elder handed the young bride into the new travelling-carriage with his stateliest grace, and Mr. and Mrs. Jacob Dolph, junior, rolled proudly up the road, through Bloomingdale, and across King's Bridge—stopping for luncheon at the Des Anges house—over to New Rochelle, where the feminine head of the house of Des Anges received them at her broad front door, and where they had the largest room in her large, old-fashioned house, for one night. Madam Des Anges wished to keep them longer, and was authoritative about it. But young Jacob settled the question of supremacy then and there, with the utmost courtesy, and Madam Des Anges, being great enough to know that she was beaten, sent off the victor on the morrow, with his trembling accomplice [68] by his side, and wished them *bon voyage* as heartily as she possibly could.

So they started afresh on their bridal tour, and very soon the travelling carriage struck the old Queen Anne's Road, and reached Yonkers. And there, and from there up to Fishkill, they passed from one country-house to another, bright particular stars at this dinner and at that supper, staying a day here and a night there, and having just the sort of sociable, public, restless, rattling good time that neither of them wanted.

At every country-house where they stayed a day they were pressed to stay a week, and always the whole neighborhood was routed out to pay them social tribute. The neighbors came in by all manner of conveyances. One family of aristocrats started at six o'clock in the morning, and travelled fourteen miles down the river in an ox-cart, the ladies sitting bolt upright, with their hair elaborately dressed for the evening's entertainment. And once a regular assembly ball was given in their honor, at a town-hall, the use of which was granted for the purpose specified by unanimous [69] vote of the town council. Of course, they had a very good time; but then there are various sorts of good times. Perhaps they might have selected another sort for themselves.

There is a story that, on their way back, they put up for several days at a poor little hostelry under the hills below Peekskill, and spent their time in wandering through the woods and picking wild-flowers; but it lacks confirmation, and I should be sorry to believe that two well-brought-up young people would prefer their own society to the unlimited hospitality of their friends in the country.

Old Jacob Dolph, at home, had the great house all to himself; and, although black Chloe took excellent care of his material comforts, he was restless and troubled. He took most pleasure in a London almanac, on whose smudgy pages he checked off the days. Letters came as often as the steamboat arrived from Albany, and he read them, after his fashion. It took him half the week to get through one missive, and by that time another had arrived. But I fear he did not make much out [70] of them. Still, they gave him one pleasure. He endorsed them carefully with the name of the writer, and the date of receipt, and then he laid them away in his desk, as neatly as he had filed his business letters in his old days of active life.

Every night he had a candle alight in the hallway; and if there were a far-off rumble of carriage-wheels late at night, he would rise from his bed—he was a light sleeper, in his age—and steal out into the corridor, hugging his dressing-robe about him, to peer anxiously down over the balusters till the last sound and the last faint hope of his son's return had died away.

And, indeed, it was late in July when the travelling-carriage once more drew up in front of the Dolph house, and old Julius opened the door, and old Mr. Dolph welcomed them, and told them that he had been very lonely in their absence, and that their mother—and then he remembered that their mother was dead, and went into the house with his head bowed low.

[TOC] [71]

## III.

St. John's Park and Hudson Street and all well-bred New York, for that matter, had its fill of the Dolph hospitality the next winter. It was dinner and ball and rout and merry-making of one sort or another, the season through. The great family sleighs and the little bachelor sleighs whirred and jingled up to the Dolph door surely two, and sometimes four, evenings in every week, and whirred and jingled away again at intensely fashionable hours, such as plain folk used for sleeping.

They woke up Abram Van Riper, did the revellers northward bound to country houses on the river-side, and, lying deep in his feather-bed, he directed his rumbling imprecations at the panes of glass, that sparkled with frost in the mild moonlight.

> "Oh, come, maidens, come, o'er the blue, rolling wave,
> The lovely should still be the care of the brave—
> Trancadillo, trancadillo, trancadillo, dillo, dillo, dillo!"

[72] sang the misguided slaves of fashion, as they sped out of hearing.

"Trancadillo!" rumbled Mr. Van Riper. "I'd like to trancadillo them, consume 'em!" and then he cursed his old friend's social circle for a parcel of trumpery fools; and Mrs. Van Riper, lying by his side, sighed softly with chastened regret and hopeless aspiration.

But everybody else—everybody who was anybody—blessed the Dolphs and the Dolphs' cellar, and their man-servant and their maid-servant, and their roasted ox and their saddle of venison, and the distinguished stranger who was within their gates; and young Mrs. Dolph was made as welcome as she made others.

For the little girl with the great dark eyes took to all this giddiness as naturally as possible—after her quiet fashion. The dark eyes sparkled with subdued pleasure that had no mean pride in it when she sat at the head of her great mahogany table, and smiled at the double row of bright faces that hemmed in the gorgeous display of the Dolph silver and china and fine linen. And it was wonderful how charming were the famous Des Anges manners, [73] when they were softened and sweetened by so much grace and beauty.

"Who would have thought she had it in her?" said the young ladies down in St. John's Park. "You remember her, don't you, what a shy little slip of a thing she was when we were at old Dumesnil's together? Who was it used to say that she had had the life grandmothered out of her?"

"Fine little creature, that wife of Dolph's," said the young men as they strolled about in Niblo's Garden. "Dolph wouldn't have had the road all to himself if that old dragon of a grandmother had given the girl half a chance. 'Gad, she's an old grenadier! They say that Dolph had to put her through her facings the day after he was married, and that he did it in uncommon fine style, too."

"He's a lucky devil, that Dolph," the younger ones would sigh. "Nothing to do, all the money he wants, pretty wife, and the best wine in New York! I wish *my* old man would cut the shop and try to get an education in wine."

Their devotion to the frivolities of fashion [74] notwithstanding, the young Dolphs were a loving, and, in a way, a domestic couple. Of course, everybody they knew had to give them a dinner or a ball, or pay them some such social tribute, and there were a myriad calls to be received and returned; but they found time for retired communings, even for long drives in the sleigh which, many a time in young Jacob Dolph's bachelor days, had borne the young man and a female companion—not always the same companion, either—up the Bloomingdale Road. And in the confidences of those early days young Jacob learned what his gentle little wife told him—without herself realizing the pathos of it—the story of her crushed, unchildlike youth, loveless till he came, her prince, her deliverer. Dolph understood it; he had known, of course, that she could not have been happy under the *régime* of Madam Des Anges; but when he heard the simple tale in all its monotonous detail, and saw spread out before him this poor young life, with its thousand little disappointments, submissions, abnegations, and undeserved punishments and needless restrictions, a generous [75] rage glowed in his heart, and perhaps sprang once in a while to his indiscreet lips; and out of this grew a deeper and maturer tenderness than his honeymoon love for the sweet little soul that he had at first sought only for the dark eyes through which it looked out upon its joyless world.

It is unwise to speak in profane language, it is injudicious to speak disrespectfully of old age, yet the Recording Angel, if he did not see fit to let a tear fall upon the page, perchance found it convenient to be mending his pen when young Jacob Dolph once uttered certain words that made his wife cry out:

"Oh, Jacob, don't, *please* don't. She didn't mean it!"

This is only a supposition. Perhaps Madam Des Anges really had meant well. But oh, how much happier this world would be if all the people who "mean well" and do ill would only take to meaning ill and doing well!

Jacob Dolph the elder took but a doubtful part in all the festivities. The cloud that had [76] hung dimly over him had begun to show little rifts; but the dark masses between the rifts were thicker and heavier than ever. It was the last brief convulsive struggle of the patient against the power of the anæsthetic, when the nervous hand goes up to put the cloth away from the mouth, just before the work is done and consciousness slips utterly away, and life [77] is no more for the sufferer, though his heart beat and the breath be warm between his lips.

When he was bright he was almost like his old self, and these delusive periods came oftenest when he met some old friend, or in quiet morning hours when his daughter—so he always called her—sat at his feet in the sunny breakfast-room, and sewed and listened, or perhaps read to him from Scott's latest novel.

He may have had some faint sub-consciousness of his condition, for although he took the deepest interest in the balls and the dinners, he would never appear before his son's guests except when he was at his best and brightest. But he loved to sit, withdrawn in a corner, watching the young life that fluttered through the great rooms, smiling to himself, and gently pleased if some old crony sought him out and talked of old times—the older the times were, the better he remembered them. Indeed, he now recalled some things that he had not thought of since his far-off boyhood.

In truth, the younger Dolphs often had small heart in their festal doings. But the [78] medical science of the day, positive, self-satisfied, and blinded by all manner of tradition, gave them, through its ministers, cruelly false hopes of the old man's ultimate recovery. Besides, they could not well order things otherwise. The extravagant hospitality of the day demanded such ceremonial, and to have abated any part of it would only have served to grieve and to alarm the object of their care.

The whole business was a constant pride and joy to old Mr. Jacob Dolph. When there was a dinner to be given, he would follow Aline as she went about the house superintending the preparations of her servants, in her flowered apron of black silk, with her bunch of keys—honest keys, those, a good four inches long, with tongues as big as a domino—jingling at her side. He would himself overlook the making ready of the wines, and give oft-repeated instructions as to the proper temperature for the port, and see that the champagne was put on ice in the huge octagonal cellaret in the dining-room corner. And when all was ready, as like as not he would kiss Aline on the forehead, and say: [79]

"I have a headache to-night, my dear, and I think I shall take my dinner in my room."

And he would go feebly up stairs, and when old Julius, who always waited upon him, brought up his tray, he would ask:

"Is it a fine dinner, Julius? Did everybody come?"

And Julius would invariably reply, with profound African dignity:

"Mons'us gran' dinneh, seh! 'E fines' dinneh I eveh witness', seh! I have stood behin' you' chai', seh, this thutty y'ah, an' I neveh see no such a gran' dinneh, Misteh Do'ph, seh!"

"Mons'us gran' dinneh, Seh!"

"Except the dinner we gave Mr. Hamilton; in State Street, Julius," the old man would put in.

"*Ex*cep' that, seh," Julius would gravely reply: "*that* was a pol-litical dinneh, seh; an', *of* co'se, a pol'litical dinneh— " an expressive pause—"but this he' is sho'ly a mons'us fine dinneh, seh."

His bodily vigor was unimpaired, however, and except that his times of entire mental clearness grew fewer and briefer as the months [80] went on, there was little change in the old gentleman when the spring of 1829 came. He was not insane, he was not idiot-ic, even at the worst. It seemed to be simply a premature old age that clouded his faculties. He forgot many things, he was weakly absent-minded, often he did not recognize a familiar face, and he seemed ever more and more disinclined to think and to talk. He liked best to sit in silence, seemingly unconscious of the world about him; and if he was aroused from his dreamy trance, his wandering speech would show that his last thought—and it might have entered his mind hours before, at the suggestion of some special event—was so far back in the past that it dealt with matters beyond his son's knowledge.

He was allowed to do as he pleased, for in the common affairs of daily life he seemed to be able to care for himself, and he plaintively resented anything that looked like guardianship. So he kept up his custom of walking down into the city, at least as far as St. Paul's. It was thought to be safe enough, for he was a familiar figure in the town, and had friends at every turn. [81]

But one afternoon he did not return in time for dinner. Young Jacob was out for his afternoon ride, which that day had taken him in the direction of the good doctor's house. And when he had reached the house, he found the doctor likewise mounted for a ride. The doctor was going up to Bond Street—the Dolphs' quarter was growing fashionable already—to look at a house near Broadway that he had some thoughts of buying, for he was to be married the coming winter. So they had ridden back together, and after a long examination of the house, young Jacob had ridden off for a gallop through the country lanes; and it was five o'clock, and dinner was on the table, when he came to his father's house and learned from tearful Aline that his father was missing.

The horse was at the stable door when young Jacob mounted him once more and galloped off to Bond Street, where he found the doctor just ready to turn down the Bowery; and they joined forces and hurried back, and down Broadway, inquiring of the people who sat on their front stoops—it was a late spring evening, [82] warm and fair—if they had seen old Mr. Dolph that day.

Many had seen him as he went down; but no one could remember that the old gentleman had come back over his accustomed path. At St. Paul's, the sexton thought that Mr. Dolph had prolonged his walk down the street. Further on, some boys had seen him, still going southward. The searchers stopped at one or two of the houses where he might have called; but there was no trace of him. It was long since old Jacob Dolph had made a formal call.

But at Bowling Green they were hailed by Mr. Philip Waters, who came toward them with more excitement in his mien than a young man of good society often exhibited.

"I was going for a carriage, Dolph," he said: "your father is down there in the Battery Park, and I'm afraid—I'm afraid he's had a stroke of paralysis."

They hurried down, and found him lying on the grass, his head on the lap of a dark-skinned, ear-ringed Spanish sailor. He had been seen to fall from the bench near by, another maritime man in the crowd about him explained. [83]

"It was only a minit or two ago," said the honest seafarer, swelled with the importance that belongs to the narrator of a tale of accident and disaster. "He was a-settin' there, had been for two hours 'most, just a-starin' at them houses over there, and all of a sudden chuck forward he went, right on his face. And then a man come along that knowed him, and said he'd go for a kerridge, or I'd 'a' took him on my sloop—she's a-layin' here now, with onions from Weathersfield—and treated him [84] well; I see he wa'n't no disrespectable character. Here, Pedro, them's the old man's folks—let 'em take him. A-settin' there nigh on two hours, he was, just a-studyin' them houses. B'long near here?"

Young Jacob had no words for the Connecticut captain. Waters had arrived, with somebody's carriage, confiscated on the highway, and they gently lifted up the old gentleman and set off homeward. They were just in time, for Waters had been the earliest of the evening promenaders to reach the Battery. It was dinner hour—or supper hour for many—and the park was given up to the lounging sailors from the river-side streets.

The doctor's face was dark.

"No, it is not paralysis," he said. "Let us proceed at once to your own home, Mr. Dolph. In view of what I am now inclined to consider his condition, I think it would be the most advisable course."

He was as precise and exact in his speech, even then, as he was later on, when years had given an innocent, genial pomposity to his delivery of his rounded sentences. [85]

They put old Jacob Dolph to bed in the room which he had always occupied, in his married as in his widowed days. He never spoke again; that day, indeed, he hardly moved. But on the next he stirred uneasily, as though he were striving to change his position. The doctor bled him, and they shifted him as best they could, but he seemed no more comfortable. So the doctor bled him again; and even that did no good.

About sunset, Aline, who had watched over him with hardly a moment's rest, left the room for a quarter of an hour, to listen to what the doctors had to say—there were four of them in the drawing-room below. When she and her husband entered the sick-room again, the old man had moved in his bed. He was lying on his side, his face to the windows that looked southward, and he had raised himself a little on his arm. There was a troubled gaze in his eyes, as of one who strains to see something that is unaccountably missing from his sight. He turned his head a little, as though to listen. Thus gazing, with an inward and spiritual vision only, at the bay that his eyes [86] might never again see, and listening to the waves whose cadence he should hear no more, the troubled look faded into one of inscrutable peace, and he sank back into the hollow of his son's arm and passed away.

The next time that the doctor was in the house it was of a snowy night a few days after New Year's Day. It was half-past two o'clock in the morning, and Jacob Dolph—no longer Jacob Dolph the younger—had been pacing furiously up and down the long dining-room—that being the longest room in the house—when the doctor came down stairs, and addressed him with his usual unruffled precision:

"I will request of you, Dolph, a large glass of port. I need not suggest to you that it is unnecessary to stint the measure, for the hospitality of this house is— —"

"How is she, doctor? For God's sake, tell me—is she—is she— —"

"The hospitality of this house is prover—" the precise doctor recommenced.

"Damn the hospitality!" cried Jacob Dolph: [87] "I mean—oh, doctor—tell me—is anything wrong?"

"Should I request of you the cup of amity and geniality, Mr. Dolph, were there cause for anything save rejoicing in this house?"

demanded the physician, with amiable severity. "I had thought that my words would have conveyed— —"

"It's all over?"

"And bravely over!" And the doctor nodded his head with a dignified cheerfulness.

"And may I go to her?"

"You may, sir, after you have given me my glass of port. But remember, sir— —"

Dolph turned to the sideboard, grasped a bottle and a glass, and thrust them into the doctor's hand, and started for the door.

"But remember, sir," went on the unperturbed physician, "you must not agitate or excite her. A gentle step, a tranquil tone, and a cheerful and encouraging address, brief and affectionate, will be all that is permitted."

Dolph listened in mad impatience, and was over the threshold before the doctor's peremptory call brought him back. [88]

"What is it now?" he demanded, impatiently.

The doctor looked at him with a gaze of wonder and reproach.

"It is a male child, sir," he said.

Jacob Dolph crept up the stairs on tiptoe. As he paused for a moment in front of a door at the head, he heard the weak, spasmodic wail of another Dolph.

"There's no help for it—I've got to do it," said Jacob Dolph.

It was another wintry morning, just after breakfast. The snow was on the ground, and [89] the sleigh-bells up in Broadway sent down a faint jingling. Ten winters had come and gone, and Mr. Dolph was as comfortably stout as a man should be who is well fed and forty.

He stood with his back to the fire, pulling at his whiskers—which formed what was earlier known as a Newgate collar—with his right thumb and forefinger. His left thumb was stuck in the armhole of his flowered satin waistcoat, black and shiny.

Opposite him sat a man of his own age, clean-shaven and sharp-featured. He had calm, somewhat cold, gray eyes, a deliberate, self-contained manner of speaking, and a pallid, dry complexion that suited with his thin features. His dress was plain, although it was thoroughly neat. He had no flowered satin waistcoat; but something in his bearing told you that he was a man who had no anxiety about the narrow things of the counting-room; who had no need to ask himself how much money was coming in to-morrow. And at the same time you felt that every cent of whatever might be to-morrow's dues would find its way to his hands as surely as the representative [90] figures stood on his ledger's page. It was young Mr. Van Riper—but he, too, had lost his right to that title, not only because of his years, but because, in the garret of the house in Greenwich Village, a cobweb stretched from one of the low beams to the head of old Abram Van Riper's great walking-stick, which stood in the corner where it had been placed, with other rubbish, the day after Abram Van Riper's funeral.

"I should not advise it, Dolph, if it can be helped," Mr. Van Riper observed, thoughtfully.

"It can't be helped."

"I can give you your price, of course," Van Riper went on, with deliberation; "but equally of course, it won't be anything like what the property will bring in the course of a few years."

Dolph kicked at the hearthrug, as he answered, somewhat testily:

"I'm not making a speculation of it."

Mr. Van Riper was unmoved.

"And I'm not making a speculation of you, either," he said, calmly: "I am speaking only for your own benefit, Dolph." [91]

Mr. Dolph put his hands in his pockets, strode to the window and back again, and then said, with an uneasy little laugh:

"I beg your pardon, Van Riper; you're quite right, of course. The fact is, I've got to do it. I must have the money, and I must have it now."

Mr. Van Riper stroked his sharp chin.

"Is it necessary to raise the money in that particular way? You are temporarily embarrassed—I don't wish to be intrusive—but why not borrow what you need, and give me a mortgage on the house?"

Ten years had given Jacob Dolph a certain floridity; but at this he blushed a hot red.

"Mortgage on the house? No, sir," he said, with emphasis.

"Well, any other security, then," was Van Riper's indifferent amendment.

Again Jacob Dolph strode to the window and back again, staring hard at the carpet, and knitting his brows.

Mr. Van Riper waited in undisturbed calm until his friend spoke once more.

"I might as well tell you the truth, Van [92] Riper," he said, at last; "I've made a fool of myself. I've lost money, and I've got to pocket the loss. As to borrowing, I've borrowed all I ought to borrow. I *won't* mortgage the house. This sale simply represents the hole in my capital."

Something like a look of surprise came into Mr. Van Riper's wintry eyes.

"It's none of my business, of course," he observed; "but if you haven't any objection to telling me——"

"What did it? What does for everybody nowadays? Western lands and Wall Street—that's about the whole story. Oh, yes, I know—I ought to have kept out of it. But I didn't. I was nothing better than a fool at such business. I'm properly punished."

He sighed as he stood on the hearthrug, his hands under his coattails, and his head hanging down. He looked as though many other thoughts were going through his mind than those which he expressed.

"I wish," he began again, "that my poor old father had brought me up to business ways. I might have kept out of it all. College is a [93] good thing for a man, of course; but college doesn't teach you how to buy lots in western cities—especially when the western cities aren't built."

"College teaches you a good many other things, though," said Van Riper, frowning slightly, as he put the tips of his long fingers together; "I wish I'd had your chance, Dolph. *My* boy shall go to Columbia, that's certain."

"*Your* boy?" queried Dolph, raising his eyebrows.

Van Riper smiled.

"Yes," he said, "my boy. You didn't know I had a boy, did you? He's nearly a year old."

This made Mr. Jacob Dolph kick at the rug once more, and scowl a little.

"I'm afraid I haven't been very neighborly, Van Riper—" he began; but the other interrupted him, smiling good-naturedly.

"You and I go different ways, Dolph," he said. "We're plain folks over in Greenwich Village, and you—you're a man of fashion."

Jacob Dolph smiled—not very mirthfully. [94] Van Riper's gaze travelled around the room, quietly curious.

"It costs money to be a man of fashion, doesn't it?"

"Yes," said Dolph, "it does."

There was silence for a minute, which Van Riper broke.

"If you've got to sell, Dolph, why, it's a pity; but I'll take it. I'll see Ogden to-day, and we can finish the business whenever you wish. But in my opinion, you'd do better to borrow."

Dolph shook his head.

"I've been quite enough of a fool," he replied.

"Well," said Mr. Van Riper, rising, "I must get to the office. You'll hear from Ogden to-morrow. I'm sorry you've got in such a snarl; but—" his lips stretched into something like a smile—"I suppose you'll know better next time. Good-day."

After Mr. Dolph had bowed his guest to the door, Mrs. Dolph slipped down the stairs and into the drawing-room. [95]

"Did he take it?" she asked.

"Of course he took it," Dolph answered, bitterly, "at that price."

"Did he say anything," she inquired again, "about its being hard for us to—to sell it?"

"He said we had better not sell it now—that it would bring more a few years hence."

"He doesn't understand," said Mrs. Dolph.

"He *couldn't* understand," said Mr. Dolph.

Then she went over to him and kissed him.

"It's only selling the garden, after all," she said; "it isn't like selling our home."

He put his arm about her waist, and they walked into the breakfast-room, and looked out on the garden which to-morrow would be theirs no longer, and in a few months would not be a garden at all.

High walls hemmed it in—the walls of the houses which had grown up around them. A few stalks stood up out of the snow, the stalks of old-fashioned flowers—hollyhock and larkspur and Job's-tears and the like—and the lines of the beds were defined by the tiny hedges of box, with the white snow-powder [96] sifted into their dark, shiny green. The bare rose-bushes were there, with their spikes of thorns, and little mounds of snow showed where the glories of the poppy-bed had bloomed.

Jacob Dolph, looking out, saw the clear summer sunlight lying where the snow lay now. He saw his mother moving about the paths, cutting a flower here and a bud there. He saw himself, a little boy in brave breeches, following her about, and looking for the harmless toads, and working each one into one of the wonderful legends which he had heard from the old German gardener across the way. He saw his father, too, pacing those paths of summer evenings, when the hollyhocks nodded their pink heads, and glancing up, from time to time, at his mother as she sat knitting at that very window. And, last of all in the line, yet first in his mind, he saw his wife tripping out in the fresh morning, to smile on the flowers she loved, to linger lovingly over the beds of verbena, and to pick the little nosegay that stood by the side of the tall coffee-urn at every summer-morning breakfast. [97]

And the wife, looking out by his side, saw that splendid boy of theirs running over path and bed, glad of the flowers and the air and the freedom, full of young life and boyish sprightliness, his long hair floating behind him, the light of hope and youth in his bright face.

And to-morrow it would be Van Riper's; and very soon there would be houses there, to close up the friendly window which had seen so much, which had let so much innocent joy and gladness into the old breakfast-room; and there would be an end of flower-bordered paths and nodding hollyhocks. She put her face upon her husband's shoulder, and cried a little, though he pretended not to know it. When she lifted it, somehow she had got her eyes dry, though they were painfully bright and large.

"It isn't like selling our house," she said.

[TOC] [98]

## IV.

Jacob Dolph got out of the Broadway stage at Bowling Green, followed by Eustace Dolph. Eustace Dolph at twenty-two was no more like his father than his patrician name was like simple and scriptural Jacob. The elder Dolph was a personable man, certainly; a handsome man, even, who looked to be nearer forty than fifty-two; and he was well dressed—perhaps a trifle out of the mode—and carried himself with a certain genial dignity, and with the lightness of a man who has not forgotten that he has been a buck in his time. But Eustace was distinctly and unmistakably a dandy. There are superficial differences, of course, between the dandy of 1852 and the dandy of 1887; but the structural foundation of all types of dandy is the same through all ages. Back of the clothes—back of the ruffles, or the bright neckcloth, or the high pickardil—which may vary with the time or the individual, you will ever find clearly displayed to [99] your eyes the obvious and unmistakable spiritual reason for and cause of the dandy—and it is always self-assertion pushed beyond the bounds of self-respect.

Now, as a matter of fact, young Eustace's garments were not really worse than many a man has worn from simple, honest bad taste. To be sure, the checked pattern of his trousers was for size like the design of a prison grating; he had a coat so blue that it shimmered in the sunlight; his necktie was of purple satin, and fearfully and wonderfully made and fringed, and decked with gems fastened by little gold chains to other inferior guardian gems; and his waistcoat was confected of satin and velvet and damask all at once; yet you might have put all these things on his father, and, although the effect would not have been pleasant, you would never have called the elder gentleman a dandy. In other words, it was why young Eustace wore his raiment that made it dandified, and not the inherent gorgeousness of the raiment itself.

The exchange of attire might readily have been made, so far as the size of the two men [100] was concerned. But only in size were they alike. There was nothing of the Dolph in Eustace's face. He bore, indeed, a strong resemblance to his maternal great-grandmother, now many years put away where she could no longer trouble the wicked, and where she had to let the weary be at rest. (And how poor little Aline had wept and wailed over that death, and lamented that she had not been more dutiful as a child!) But his face was not strong, as the face of Madam Des Anges had been. Some strain of a weaker ancestry reappeared in it, and, so to speak, changed the key of the expression. What had been pride in the old lady bordered on superciliousness in the young man. What had been sternness became a mere haughtiness. Yet it was a handsome face, and pleasant, too, when the young smile came across it, and you saw the white small teeth and the bright, intelligent light in the dark eyes.

The two men strolled through the Battery, and then up South Street, and so around through Old Slip. They were on business; but this was also a pleasure trip to the elder. He walked doubly in spirit through those old [101] streets—a boy by his father's side, a father with his son at his elbow. He had not been often in the region of late years. You remember, he was a man of pleasure. He was one of the first-fruits of metropolitan growth and social culture. His father had made an idler and *dilettante* of him. It was only half a life at best, he thought, happy as he had been; blessed as he was in wife and child. He was going to make a business man of his own boy. After all, it was through the workers that great cities grew. Perhaps we were not ripe yet for that European institution, the idler. He himself had certain accomplishments that other Americans had not. He could *flâner*, for instance. But to have to *flâner* through fifty or sixty or seventy years palled on the spirit, he found. And one thing was certain, if any Dolph was ever to be an accomplished *flâneur*, and to devote his whole life to that occupation, the Dolph fortune must be vastly increased. Old Jacob Dolph had miscalculated. The sum he had left in 1829 might have done very well for the time, but it was no fortune to idle on among the fashionables of 1852. [102]

Something of this Mr. Dolph told his son; but the young man, although he listened with respectful attention, appeared not to take a deep interest in his father's reminiscences. Jacob Dolph fancied even that Eustace did not care to be reminded of the city's day of small things. Perhaps he had something of the feeling of the successful struggler who tries to forget the shabbiness of the past. If this were the case, his pride must have been chafed, for his father was eloquent in displaying the powers of an uncommonly fine memory;

and he had to hear all about the slips, and the Fly Market, and the gradual extension of the water-front, and the piles on which the old Tontine was built, and the cucumber-wood pipes of the old water-company, still lying under their feet. Once, at least, he showed a genuine enjoyment of his father's discourse, and that was when it ran on the great retinue of servants in which Jacob Dolph the elder had indulged himself. I think he was actually pleased when he heard that his grandfather had at one time kept slaves.

Wandering in this way, to the running accompaniment [103] of Mr. Dolph's lecture, they came to Water Street, and here, as though he were reminded of the object of their trip, the father summed up his reminiscences in shape for a neat moral.

"The city grows, you see, my boy, and we've got to grow with it. I've stood still; but you sha'n't."

"Well, governor," said the younger man, "I'll be frank with you. I don't like the prospect."

"You will—you will, my boy. You'll live to thank me."

"Very likely you're right, sir; I don't deny it; but, as I say, I don't like the prospect. I don't see—with all due respect, sir—how any gentleman can *like* trade. It may be necessary, and of course I don't think it's lowering, or any of that nonsense, you know; but it can't be *pleasant*. Of course, if *your* governor had to do it, it was all right; but I don't believe he liked it any better than I should, or he wouldn't have been so anxious to keep you out of it."

"My poor father made a great mistake, [104] Eustace. He would admit it now, I'm sure, if he were alive."

"Well, sir, I'm going to try it, of course. I'll give it a fair trial. But when the two years are up, sir, as we agreed, I hope you won't say anything against my going into the law, or—well, yes—" he colored a little—"trying what I can do on the Street. I know what you think about it, sir," he went on, hastily; "but there are two sides to the question, and it's my opinion that, for an intelligent man, there's more money to be made up there in Wall Street in one year than can be got out of haggling over merchandise for a lifetime."

Jacob Dolph grew red in the face and shook his head vigorously.

"Don't speak of it, sir, don't speak of it!" he said, vehemently. "It's the curse of the country. If you have any such infernal opinions, don't vent them in my presence, sir. I know what I am talking about. Keep clear of Wall Street, sir. It is the straight road to perdition."

They entered one of a row of broad-fronted buildings of notable severity and simplicity of [105] architecture. Four square stone columns upheld its brick front, and on one of these faded gilt letters, on a ground of dingy black, said simply:

**ABRAM VAN RIPER'S SON.**

There was no further announcement of Abram Van Riper's Son's character, or of the nature of his business. It was assumed that all people knew who Abram Van Riper's Son was, and that his (Abram Van Riper's) ship-chandlery trade had long before grown into a great "commission merchant's" business.

It was full summer, and there were no doors between the pillars to bar entrance to the gloomy cavern behind them, which stretched in semi-darkness the whole length and width of the building, save for a narrow strip at the rear, where, behind a windowed partition, clerks were writing at high desks, and where there was an inner and more secluded pen for Abram Van Riper's son.

In the front of the cave, to one side, was a hoistway, where bales and boxes were drawn up from the cellar or swung twisting and twirling [106] to the lofts above. Amidships the place was strewn with small tubs, matting-covered bales and boxes, coils of bright new rope, and odd-looking packages of a hundred sorts, all of them with gaping wounds in their envelopes, or otherwise having their pristine integrity wounded. From this it was not difficult to

guess that these were samples of merchandise. Most of them gave forth odors upon the air, odors ranging from the purely aromatic, suggestive of Oriental fancies or tropic dreams of spice, to the positively offensive—the latter varieties predominating.

But certain objects upon a long table were so peculiar in appearance that the visitors could not pass them by with a mere glance of wonder. They looked like small leather pies, badly warped in the baking. A clerk in his [107] shirt sleeves, with his straw hat on one side of his head, whistled as he cut into these, revealing a livid interior, the color of half-cooked veal, which he inspected with care. Eustace was moved to positive curiosity.

"What are they?" he inquired of the clerk, pride mingling with disgust in his tone, as he caught a smell like unto the smell which might arise from raw smoked salmon that had lain three days in the sun.

"Central American," responded the clerk, with brevity, and resumed his whistling of

"My name is Jake Keyser, I was born in Spring Garden;
To make me a preacher my father did try."

"Central American *what*?" pursued the inquirer.

"*Rubber!*" said the clerk, with a scorn so deep and far beyond expression that the combined pride of the Dolphs and the Des Anges wilted into silence for the moment. As they went on toward the rear office, while the clerk gayly whistled the notes of

"It's no use a-blowing, for I am a hard 'un—
I'm bound to be a butcher, by heavens, or die!"

[108] Eustace recovered sufficiently to demand of his father:

"I say, sir, shall I have to handle that damned stuff?"

"Hush!" said his senior; "here's Mr. Van Riper."

Mr. Van Riper came to the office door to welcome them, with his thin face set in the form of a smile.

"Ah!" he said, "here's the young man, is he? Fine big fellow, Dolph. Well, sir, so you are going to embrace a mercantile career, are you? That's what they call it in these fine days, Dolph."

"I am going to try to, sir," replied the young man.

"He will, Van Riper," put in his father, hastily; "he'll like it as soon as he gets used to it—I know he will."

"Well," returned Mr. Van Riper, with an attempt at facetious geniality, "we'll try to get his nose down to the grindstone, we will. Come into my office with me, Dolph, and I'll hand this young gentleman over to old Mr. Daw. Mr. Daw will feel his teeth—eh, Mr. [109] Daw?—see what he *doesn't* know—how's that, Mr. Daw? You remember Mr. Daw, Dolph—used to be with your father before he went out of business—been with us ever since. Let's see, how long is that, Daw? Most fifty years, ain't it?"

Mr. Daw, who looked as though he might have been one hundred years at the business, wheeled around and descended with stiff deliberation from his high stool, holding his pen in his mouth as he solemnly shook hands with Jacob Dolph, and peered into his face. Then he took the pen out of his mouth.

"Looks like his father," was Mr. Daw's comment.

"Looks like his father," was Mr. Daw's comment. "Forty-five years the twenty-ninth of this month, sir. You was a little shaver then. I remember you comin' into the store and whittlin' timber with your little jack-knife. I was only eleven years with your father, sir—eleven years and six months—went to him when I was fourteen years old. That's fifty-six years and six months in the service of two of the best houses that ever was in New York—an' I can do my work with any two young shavers in the town—ain't missed a day in nineteen [110] years now. Your father hadn't never ought to have gone out of business, Mr. Dolph. He did a great business for those days, and he had the makin' of a big house. Goin' to bring your boy up like a good New York merchant, hey? Come along here with me, young man, and I'll see if you're half the man your grandfather was. He hadn't never ought to have given up business, Mr. Dolph. But he was all for pleasuring an' the play-houses, an' havin' fine times. Come along, young man. What's your name?"

"Eustace Dolph."

"Hm! Jacob's better."

And he led the neophyte away.

"Curious old case," said Mr. Van Riper, dryly. "Best accountant in New York. See that high stool of his?—can't get him off it. Five years ago I gave him a low desk and an arm-chair. In one week he was back again, roosting up there. Said he didn't feel comfortable with his feet on the ground. He thought that sort of thing might do for aged people, but *he* wasn't made of cotton-batting." [111]

Thus began Eustace Dolph's apprenticeship to business, and mightily ill he liked it.

There came a day, a winter day in 1854, when there was great agitation among what were then called the real old families of New York. I cannot use the term "fashionable society," because that is more comprehensive, and would include many wealthy and ambitious families from New England, who were decidedly not of the Dolphs' set. And then, the Dolphs could hardly be reckoned among the leaders of fashion. To live on or near the boundaries of fashion's domain is to lower your social status below the absolute pitch of perfection, and fashion in 1854 drew the line pretty sharply at Bleecker Street. Above Bleecker Street the cream of the cream rose to the surface; below, you were ranked as skim milk. The social world was spreading up into the wastes sacred to the circus and the market-garden, although, if Admiral Farragut had stood on his sea-legs where he stands now, he might have had a fairly clear view of Chelsea [112] Village, and seen Alonzo Cushman II., or Alonzo Cushman III., perhaps, going around and collecting his rents.

But the old families still fought the tide of trade, many of them neck-deep and very uncomfortable. They would not go from St. John's Park, nor from North Moore and Grand Streets. They had not the *bourgeois* conservatism of the Greenwich Villagers, which has held them in a solid phalanx almost to this very day; but still, in a way, they resented the up-town movement, and resisted it. So that when they did have to buy lots in the high-numbered streets they had to pay a fine price for them.

It was this social party that was stirred by a bit of scandal about the Dolphs. I do not know why I should call it scandal; yet I am sure society so held it. For did not society whisper it, and nod and wink over it, and tell it in dark corners, and chuckle, and lift its multitudinous hands and its myriad eyebrows, and say in innumerable keys: "Well, *upon* my word!" and "Well, I *should* think——!" and "Who would *ever* have thought of such a [113] thing?" and the like? Did not society make very funny jokes about it, and did not society's professional gossips get many an invitation to dinner because they professed to have authentic details of the way Mr. and Mrs. Dolph looked when they spoke about it, and just what they had to say for themselves?

And yet it was nothing more than this, that Mr. Dolph being fifty-four, and his wife but a few years younger, were about to give to the world another Dolph. It was odd, I admit; it was unusual; if I must go so far, it was, I suppose, unconventional. But I don't see that it was necessary for Mr. Philip Waters to make an epigram about it. It was a very clever epigram; but if you had seen dear old Mrs. Dolph, with her rosy cheeks and the gray in her hair, knitting baby-clothes with hands which were still white and plump and comely, while great dark eyes looked timorously into the doubtful, fear-clouded future, I think you would have been ashamed that you had even listened to that epigram.

The expected event was of special and personal interest to only three people—for, after [114] all, when you think of it, it was not exactly society's business—and it affected them in widely different ways.

Jacob Dolph was all tenderness to his wife, and all sympathy with her fears, with her nervous apprehensions, even with her morbid forebodings of impossible ills. He did not repine at the seclusion which the situation forced upon them, although his life for years had been given up to society's demands, until pleasure-seeking and pleasure-giving had grown into a routine, which occupied his whole mind. His wife saw him more than she had for many years. Clubs and card-parties had few temptations for him now; he sat at home and read to her and talked to her, and did his best to follow the injunctions of the doctor, and "create and preserve in her a spirit of cheerful and hopeful tranquillity, free of unnecessary apprehension."

But when he *did* go to the club, when he was in male society, his breast expanded, and if he had to answer a polite inquiry as to Mrs. Dolph's general health, I am afraid that he responded: "Mrs. Dolph is extremely well, sir, [115] extremely well!" with a pride which the moralists will tell you is baseless, unworthy, and unreasonable.

As for Aline herself, no one may know what timorous hopes stirred in her bosom and charmed the years away, and brought back to her a lovely youth that was almost girlish in its innocent, half-frightened gladness. Outside, this great, wise, eminently proper world that she lived in girded at the old woman who was to bear a child, and laughed behind tasselled fans, and made wondrous merry over Nature's work; but within the old house she sat, and sewed upon the baby-clothes, or, wandering from cupboard to cupboard, found the yellowing garments, laid away more than a score of years before—the poor little lace-decked trifles that her first boy had worn; and she thanked heaven, in her humble way, that twenty-four years had not taken the love and joy of a wife and a mother out of her heart.

She could not find all her boy's dresses and toys, for she was open-handed, and had given many of them away to people who needed them. This brought about an odd encounter. [116] The third person who had a special interest in the prospect of the birth of a Dolph was young Eustace, and he found nothing in it wherewith to be pleased. For Eustace Dolph was of the ultra-fashionables. He cared less for old family than for new ideas, and he did not let himself fall behind in the march of social progress, even though he was, as he admitted with humility born of pride, only a poor devil of a down-town clerk. If his days were occupied, he had his nights to himself, and he lengthened them to suit himself. At first this caused his mother to fret a little; but poor Aline had come into her present world from the conventional seclusion of King's Bridge, and her only authority on questions of masculine license was her husband. He, being appealed to, had to admit that his own hours in youth had been late, and that he supposed the hours of a newer generation should properly be later still. Mr. Dolph forgot, perhaps, that while his early potations had been vinous, those of the later age were distinctly spirituous; and that the early morning cocktail and the midnight brandy-and-soda were abominations unknown to his own [117] well-bred youth. With port and sherry and good Bordeaux he had been familiar all his life; a dash of *liqueur* after dinner did not trouble his digestion; he found a bottle of champagne a pleasant appetizer and a gentle stimulant; but whiskey and gin were to him the drinks of the vulgar; and rum and brandy stood on his sideboard only to please fiercer tastes than his own. Perhaps, also, he was ignorant of the temptations that assail a young man in a great city, he who had grown up in such a little one that he had at one time known every one who was worth knowing in it.

However this may have been, Eustace Dolph ruled for himself his going out and his coming in. He went further, and chose his own associates, not always from among the scions of the "old families." He found those excellent young men "slow," and he selected for his own private circle a set which was mixed as to origin and unanimously frivolous as to tendency. The foreign element was strongly represented. Bright young Irishmen of excellent families, and mysterious French and Italian counts and marquises, borrowed [118] many of the good gold dollars of the Dolphs, and forgot to return an equivalent in the local currency of the O'Reagans of Castle Reagan, or the D'Arcy de Montmorenci, or

the Montescudi di Bajocchi. Among this set there was much merry-making when the news from the Dolph household sifted down to them from the gossip-sieve of the best society. They could not very well chaff young Dolph openly, for he was muscular and high-tempered, and, under the most agreeable conditions, needed a fight of some sort every six months or so, and liked a bit of trouble in between fights. But a good deal of low and malicious humor came his way, from one source or another, and he, with the hot and concentrated egotism of youth, thought that he was in a ridiculous and trying position, and chafed over it.

There had been innuendos and hints and glancing allusions, but no one had dared to make any direct assault of wit, until one evening [119] young Haskins came into the club "a little flushed with wine." (The "wine" was brandy.) It seems that young Haskins had found at home an ivory rattle which had belonged to Eustace twenty years before, and which Mrs. Dolph had given to Mrs. Haskins when Eustace enlarged his horizon in the matter of toys.

Haskins, being, as I have said, somewhat flushed with brandy, came up to young Dolph, who was smoking in the window, and meditating with frowning brows, and said to him:

"Here, Dolph, I've done with this. You'd better take it back—it may be wanted down your way."

There was a scene. Fortunately, two men were standing just behind Dolph, who were able to throw their arms about him, and hold him back for a few seconds. There would have been further consequences, however, if it had not been that Eustace was in the act of throwing the rattle back at Haskins when the two men caught him. Thus the toy went wide of its mark, and fell in the lap of Philip Waters, who, old as he was, generally chose to [120] be in the company of the young men at the club; and then Philip Waters did something that almost atones, I think, for the epigram.

He looked at the date on the rattle, and then he rose up and went between the two young men, and spoke to Haskins.

"Young man," he said, "when Mrs. Jacob Dolph gave your mother this thing, your father had just failed for the second time in three years. He had come to New York about five years before from Hartford, or Providence, or—Succotash, or whatever his confounded town was. Mr. Jacob Dolph got Mr. Van Riper to give your father an extension on his note, or he would have gone to the debtors' prison down by the City Hall. As it was, he had to sell his house, and the coat off his back, for all I know. If it hadn't been for the Dolphs, devil the rattle you'd have had, and you wouldn't have been living in Bond Street to-day."

"If it hadn't been for the Dolphs, devil the rattle you'd have had."

After which Mr. Philip Waters sat down and read the evening paper; and when young Haskins was able to speak he asked young Dolph's pardon, and got it—at least, a formal assurance that he had it. [121]

The baby was born in the spring, and everybody said she was the image of her mother.

There will come a day, it may be, when advancing civilization will civilize sleighing out of existence, as far as New York is concerned. Year after year the days grow fewer that will let a cutter slip up beyond the farthest of the "road-houses" and cross the line into Westchester. People say that the climate is changing; but close observers recognize a sympathy between the decrease of snow-storms and the increase of refinement—that is, a sympathy in inverse ratio; a balanced progress in opposite directions. As we grow further and further beyond even old-world standards of polite convention, as we formalize and super-formalize our codes, and steadily eliminate every element of amusement from our amusements, Nature in strict conformity represses her joyous exuberance. The snow-storm of the past is gone, because the great public sleigh that held twenty-odd merry-makers in a shell like a circus band-wagon has gone out of fashion [122] among all classes. Now we have, during severe winters, just enough snow from time to time to bear the light sleigh of the young man who, being in good society, is also horsy. When *he* finds the road vulgar, the poor plebeian souls who go sleighing for the sport of it may sell their red and blue vehicles, for Nature, the sycophant of fashion, will snow no more.

But they had "good old-fashioned" snow-storms eighty years after the Declaration of Independence, and one had fallen upon New York that tempted Mrs. Jacob Dolph to leave her baby, ten months old, in the nurse's charge, and go out with her husband in the great family sleigh for what might be the last ride of the season.

They had been far up the road—to Arcularius's, maybe, there swinging around and whirling back. They had flown down the long country road, and back into the city, to meet—it was early in the day—the great procession of sleighing folk streaming northward up Broadway. It was one of New York's great, irregular, chance-set carnivals, and every sleigh was out, from the "exquisite's" gilded chariot, [123] a shell hardly larger than a fair-sized easy-chair, to the square, low-hung red sledge of the butcher-boy, who braved it with the fashionables, his *Schneider*-made clothes on his burly form, and his girl by his side, in her best Bowery bonnet. Everybody was a-sleighing. The jingle of countless bells fell on the crisp air in a sort of broken rhythm—a rude *tempo rubato*. It was fashionable then. But we—we amuse ourselves less boisterously.

They drew up at the door of the Dolph house, and Jacob Dolph lifted his wife out of the sleigh, and carried her up the steps into the breakfast-room, and set her down in her easy-chair. He was bending over her to ask her if her ride had done her good, when a servant entered and handed him a letter marked "Immediate."

He read it, and all the color of the winter's day faded out of his face.

"I've got to go down to Van Riper's," he said, "at once; he wants me."

"Has anything happened to—to Eustace?" his wife cried out.

"He doesn't say so—I suppose—I suppose [124] it's only business of some sort," her husband said. His face was white. "Don't detain me, dear. I'll come back as soon as—as soon as I get through."

He kissed her, and was gone. Half an hour later he sat in the office of Abram Van Riper's Son.

There was no doubting it, no denying it, no palliating it even. The curse had come upon the house of Jacob Dolph, and his son was a thief and a fugitive.

It was an old story and a simple story. It was the story of the Haskins's million and the Dolphs' hundred thousand; it was the story of the boy with a hundred thousand in prospect trying to spend money against the boy with a million in sight. It was the story of cards, speculation—another name for that sort of gambling which is worse than any on the green cloth—and what is euphemistically known as wine.

There was enough oral and documentary evidence to make the whole story hideously clear to Jacob Dolph, as he sat in that dark little pen of Van Riper's and had the history [125] of his son's fall spelled out to him, word by word. The boy had proved himself apt and clever in his office work. His education had given him an advantage over all the other clerks, and he had learned his duties with wonderful ease. And when, six months before, old Mr. Daw had let himself down from his stool for the last time, and had muffled up his thin old throat in his great green worsted scarf, and had gone home to die, young Dolph had been put temporarily in his place. In those six months he had done his bad work. Even Van Riper admitted that it must have been a sudden temptation. But—he had yielded. In those six months fifty thousand dollars of Abram Van Riper's money had gone into the gulf that yawned in Wall Street; fifty thousand dollars, not acquired by falsifying the books, but filched outright from the private safe to which he had access; fifty thousand dollars, in securities which he had turned into money, acting as the confidential man of the house.

When Jacob Dolph, looking like a man of eighty, left the private office of Mr. Van [126] Riper he had two things to do. One was to tell his wife, the other was to assign enough property to Van Riper to cover the amount of the defalcation. Both had been done before night.

[TOC] [127]

## V.

It is to be said for society that there was very little chuckling and smiling when this fresh piece of news about the Dolphs came out. Nor did the news pass from house to house like wildfire. It rather leaked out here and there, percolating through barriers of friendly silence, slipping from discreet lips and repeated in anxious confidence, with all manner of qualifications and hopeful suppositions and suggestions. As a matter of fact, people never really knew just what Eustace Dolph had done, or how far his wrong-doing had carried him. All that was ever positively known was that the boy had got into trouble down-town, and had gone to Europe. The exact nature of the trouble could only be conjectured. The very brokers who had been the instruments of young Dolph's ruin were not able to separate his authorized speculations from those which were illegitimate. They could do no more than guess, from what they knew of Van Riper's [128] conservative method of investment, that the young man's unfortunate purchases were made for himself, and they figured these at fifty-five thousand odd hundred dollars.

Somebody, who looked up the deed which Jacob Dolph executed that winter day, found that he had transferred to Van Riper real estate of more than that value.

No word ever came from the cold lips of Abram Van Riper's son; and his office was a piece of all but perfect machinery, which dared not creak when he commanded silence. And no one save Van Riper and Dolph, and their two lawyers, knew the whole truth. Dolph never even spoke about it to his wife, after that first night. It was these five people only who knew that Mr. Jacob Dolph had parted with the last bit of real estate that he owned, outside of his own home, and they knew that his other property was of a doubtful sort, that could yield at the best only a very limited income—hardly enough for a man who lived in so great a house, and whose doors were open to all his friends nine months in the year.

Yet he stayed there, and grew old with an [129] age which the years have not among their gifts. When his little girl was large enough to sit upon his knee, her small hands clutched at a snowy-white mustache, and she complained that his great, dark, hollow eyes never would look "right into hers, away down deep." Yet he loved her, and talked more to her perhaps than to any one else, not even excepting Aline.

But he never spoke to her of the elder brother whom she could not remember. It was her mother who whispered something of the story to her, and told her not to let papa know that she knew of it, for it would grieve him. Aline herself knew nothing about the boy save that he lived, and lived a criminal. Jacob himself could only have told her that their son was a wandering adventurer, known as a blackleg and sharper in every town in Europe.

The doors of the great house were closed to all the world, or opened only for some old friend, who went away very soon out of the presence of a sadness beyond all solace of words, or kindly look, or hand-clasp. And so, in something that only the grace of their gentle [130] lives relieved from absolute poverty, those three dwelt in the old house, and let the world slip by them.

There was no sleep for any one of the little household in the great house on the night of the 14th of July, 1863. Doors and blinds were closed; only a light shone through the half-open slats at a second-story window, and in that room Aline lay sick, almost unto death, her white hair loosed from its usual dainty neatness, her dark eyes turning with an unmeaning gaze from the face of the little girl at her side to the face of her husband at the foot of her bed. Her hands, wrinkled and small, groped over the coverlet, with nervous twitchings, as every now and then the howls or the pistol-shots of the mob in the streets below them fell on her ear. And at every such movement the lips of the girl by her pillow twitched in piteous sympathy. About half-past twelve there was sharp firing in volleys to the southward of them, that threw the half-conscious sufferer into an agony of supersensitive disturbance. [131] Then there came a silence that seemed unnaturally deep, yet it was only the silence of a summer night in the deserted city streets.

Through it they heard, sharp and sudden, with something inexplicably fearful about it, the patter of running feet. They had heard that sound often enough that night and the night before; but these feet stopped at their own door, and came up the steps, and the runner beat and pounded on the heavy panels.

Father and child looked in each other's eyes, and then Jacob Dolph left his post at the foot of the bed, and, passing out of the room, went down the stairs with deliberate tread, and opened the door.

A negro's face, almost gray in its mad fear, stared into his with a desperate appeal which the lips could not utter. Dolph drew the man in, and shut the door behind him. The negro leaned, trembling and exhausted, against the wall.

"I knowed you'd take me in, Mist' Dolph," he panted; "I'm feared they seen me, though—they was mighty clost behind."

They were close behind him, indeed. In [132] half a minute the roar of the mob filled the street with one terrible howl and shriek of animal rage, heard high above the tramp of half a thousand feet; and the beasts of disorder, gathered from all the city's holes and dens of crime, wild for rapine and outrage, burst upon them, sweeping up the steps, hammering at the [133] great doors, crying for the blood of the helpless and the innocent.

Foreign faces, almost all! Irish, mostly; but there were heavy, ignorant German types of feature uplifted under the gas-light; sallow, black-mustached Magyar faces; thin, acute, French faces—all with the stamp of old-world ignorance and vice upon them.

The door opened, and the white-haired old gentleman, erect, haughty, with brightening eyes, faced the leader of the mob—a great fellow, black-bearded, who had a space to himself on the stoop, and swung his broad shoulders from side to side.

"Have you got a nigger here?"

"Have you got a nigger here?" he began, and then stopped short, for Jacob Dolph was looking upon the face of his son.

Vagabond and outcast, he had the vagabond's quick wit, this leader of infuriate crime, and some one good impulse stirred in him of his forfeited gentlehood. He turned savagely upon his followers.

"He ain't here!" he roared. "I told you so—I saw him turn the corner."

"Shtap an' burrn the bondholder's house!" [134] yelled a man behind. Eustace Dolph turned round with a furious, threatening gesture.

"You damned fool!" he thundered; "he's no bondholder—he's one of *us*. Go on, I tell you! Will you let that nigger get away?"

He half drove them down the steps. The old man stepped out, his face aflame under his white hair, his whole frame quivering.

"You lie, sir!" he cried; but his voice was drowned in the howl of the mob as it swept around the corner, forgetting all things else in the madness of its hideous chase.

When Jacob Dolph returned to his wife's chamber, her feeble gaze was lifted to the ceiling. At the sound of his footsteps she let it fall dimly upon his face. He was thankful that, in that last moment of doubtful quickening, she could not read his eyes; and she passed away, smiling sweetly, one of her white old hands in his, and one in her child's.

Age takes small account of the immediate flight of time. To the young, a year is a [135] mighty span. Be it a happy or an unhappy year that youth looks forward to, it is a vista that stretches far into the future. And when it is done, this interminable year, and youth, just twelve months older, looks back to the first of it, what a long way off it is! What tremendous progress we have made! How much more we know! How insufficient are the standards by which we measured the world a poor three hundred and sixty-five days back!

But age has grown habituated to the flight of time. Years? we have seen so many of them that they make no great impression upon us. What! is it ten years since young Midas first came to the counting-room, asking humbly for an entry-clerk's place—he who is now the head of the firm? Bless us! it seems like yesterday. Is it ten years since we first put on that coat? Why, it must be clean out of the fashion by this time.

But age does not carry out the thought, and ask if itself be out of the fashion. Age knows better. A few wrinkles, a stoop in the back, a certain slowness of pace, do not make a man [136] old at sixty—nor at seventy, neither; for now you come to think of it, the ten years we were speaking of is gone, and it is seventy now, and not sixty. Seventy! Why, 'tis not to be thought of as old age—save when it may be necessary to rebuke the easy arrogance of youth.

The time had come to Jacob Dolph when he could not feel that he was growing old. He was old, of course, in one sense. He was sixty-one when the war broke out; and they had not allowed him to form a regiment and go to the front at its head. But what was old for a soldier in active service was not old for a well-preserved civilian. True, he could never be the same man again, now that poor Aline was gone. True, he was growing more and more disinclined for active exercise, and he regretted he had led so sedentary a life. But though '64 piled itself up on '63, and '65 on top of that, these arbitrary divisions of time seemed to him but trivial.

Edith was growing old, perhaps; getting to be a great girl, taller than her mother and fairer of complexion, yet not unlike [137] her, he sometimes thought, as she began to manage the affairs of the house, and to go about the great shabby mansion with her mother's keys jingling at her girdle. For the years went on crawling one over the other, and soon it was 1873, and Edith was eighteen years old.

One rainy day in this year found Jacob Dolph in Wall Street. Although he himself did not think so, he was an old man to others, and kindly hands, such as were to be found even in that infuriate crowd, had helped him up the marble steps of the Sub-Treasury and had given him lodgment on one of the great blocks of marble that dominate the street. From where he stood he could see Wall Street, east and west, and the broad plaza of Broad Street to the south, filled with a compact mass of men, half hidden by a myriad of umbrellas, rain-soaked, black, glinting in the dim light. So might a Roman legion have looked, when each man raised his targum above his head and came shoulder to shoulder with his neighbor for the assault.

There was a confused, ant-like movement in [138] the vast crowd, and a dull murmur came from it, rising, in places, into excited shouts. Here and there the fringe of the mass swelled up and swept against the steps of some building, forcing, or trying to force, an entry. Sometimes a narrow stream of men trickled into the half-open doorway; sometimes the great portals closed, and then there was a mad outcry and a low groan, and the foremost on the steps suddenly turned back, and in some strange way slipped through the throng and sped in all directions to bear to hushed or clamorous offices the news that this house or that bank had "suspended payment." "Busted," the panting messengers said to white-faced merchants; and in the slang of the street was conveyed the message of doom. The great panic of 1873 was upon the town—the outcome of long years of unwarranted self-confidence, of selfish extravagance, of conscienceless speculation—and, as hour after hour passed by, fortunes were lost in the twinkling of an eye, and the bread was taken out of the mouths of the helpless.

After Jacob Dolph had stood for some time, [139] looking down upon the tossing sea of black umbrellas, he saw a narrow lane made through the crowd in the wake of a little party of clerks and porters, bearing aid perhaps to some stricken bank. Slipping down, he followed close behind them. Perhaps the jostling hundreds on the sidewalk were gentle with him, seeing that he was an old man; perhaps the strength of excitement nerved him, for he made his way down the street to the flight of steps leading to the door of a tall white building, and he crowded himself up among the pack that was striving to enter. He had even got so far that he could see the line pouring in above his head, when there was a sudden cessation of motion in the press, and one leaf of the outer iron doors swung forward, meeting the other, already closed to bar the crush, and two green-painted panels stood, impassable, between him and the last of the Dolph fortune.

One howl and roar, and the crowd turned back on itself, and swept him with it. In five minutes a thousand offices knew of the greatest failure of the day; and Jacob Dolph was [140] leaning—weak, gasping, dazed—against the side wall of a hallway in William Street, with two stray office-boys staring at him out of their small, round, unsympathetic eyes.

Let us not ask what wild temptation led the old man back again to risk all he owned in that hellish game that is played in the narrow street. We may remember this: that he saw his daughter growing to womanhood in that silent and almost deserted house, shouldered now by low tenements and wretched shops and vile drinking-places; that he may have pictured for her a brighter life in that world that had long ago left him behind it in his bereaved and disgraced loneliness; that he had had some vision of her young beauty fulfilling its destiny amid sweeter and fairer surroundings. And let us not forget that he knew no other means than these to win the money for which he cared little; which he found absolutely needful.

After Jacob Dolph had yielded for the last time to the temptation that had conquered him once before, and had ruined his son's soul; after that final disastrous battle with the [141] gamblers of Wall Street, wherein he lost the last poor remnant of the great Dolph fortune, giving up with it his father's home forever, certain old bread of his father's casting came back to him upon strange waters.

Abram Van Riper came to the daughter of the house of Dolph, a little before it became certain that the house must be sold, and told her, in his dry way, that he had to make a business communication to her, for he feared that her father was hardly capable of understanding such matters any longer. She winced [142] a little; but he took a load off her heart when he made his slow, precise explanation. The fact was, he said, that the business transactions between her father and himself, consequent upon the defalcation of her brother Eustace, had never been closed, in all these seventeen years. (Edith Dolph trembled.) It was known at the time that the property transferred by her father rather more than covered the amount of her brother's—peculation. But her father's extreme sensitiveness had led him to avoid a precise adjustment, and as the property transferred was subject to certain long leases, he, Mr. Van Riper, had thought it best to wait until the property was sold and the account closed, to settle the matter with Mr. Dolph. This had lately been done, and Mr. Van Riper found that, deducting charges, and interest on his money at seven per cent., he had made by the transaction six thousand three hundred and seventy dollars. This sum, he thought, properly belonged to Mr. Dolph. And if Miss Dolph would take the counsel of an old friend of her father's, she would leave the sum in charge of [143] the house of Abram Van Riper's Son. The house would invest it at ten per cent.—he stopped and looked at Edith, but she only answered him with innocent eyes of attention—and would pay her six hundred and thirty-seven dollars annually in quarterly payments. It might be of assistance to Mr. Dolph in his present situation.

It was of assistance. They lived on it, father and daughter, with such aid as Decorative Art—just introduced to this country—gave in semi-remunerative employment for her deft fingers.

Abram Van Riper, when he left the weeping, grateful girl, marched out into the street, turned his face toward what was once Greenwich Village, and said to his soul:

"I think that will balance any obligation my father may have put himself under in buying that State Street house too cheap. Now then, old gentleman, you can lie easy in your grave. The Van Ripers ain't beholden to the Dolphs, that's sure."

A few years ago—shall we say as many as [144] ten?—there were two small rooms up in a quiet street in Harlem, tenanted by an old gentleman and a young gentlewoman; and in the front room, which was the young woman's room by night, but a sort of parlor or sitting-room 

in the daytime, the old gentleman stood up, four times a year, to have his collar pulled up, and his necktie set right, and his coat dusted off by a pair of small white hands, so that he might be presentable when he went down town to collect certain moneys due him.

They were small rooms, but they were bright and cheerful, being decorated with sketches and studies of an artistic sort, which may have been somewhat crude and uncertain as to treatment, but were certainly pleasant and feminine. Yet few saw them save the young woman and the old man. The most [145] frequent visitor was a young artist from the West, who often escorted Miss Dolph to and from the Art League rooms. His name was Rand; he had studied in Munich; he had a future before him, and was making money on his prospects. He might just as well have lived in luxurious bachelor quarters in the lower part of the city; but, for reasons of his own, he preferred to live in Harlem.

Old Mr. Dolph insisted on going regularly every quarter-day to the office of the Van Riper Estate, "to collect," as he said, "the interest due him." Four times a year he went down town on the Eighth

Avenue cars, where the conductors soon learned to know him by his shiny black broadcloth coat and his snow-white hair. His daughter was always uneasy about these trips; but her father could not be dissuaded from them. To him they were his one hold on active life—the all-important events of the year. It would have broken his tender old heart to tell him that he could not go to collect his "interest." And so she set his necktie right, and he went.

When he got out of the car at Abingdon [146] Square he tottered, in his slow, old way, to a neat structure which combined modern jauntiness with old-time solidity, and which was labelled simply: "Office of the Van Riper Estate," and there he told the smilingly indulgent clerk that he thought he would "take it in cash, this time," and, taking it in cash, went forth.

And then he walked down through Greenwich Village into New York city, and into the street where stood the house that his father had built. Thus he had gone to view it four times a year, during every year save the first, since he had given it up.

He had seen it go through one stage of decadence after another. First it was rented, by its new owner, to the Jewish pawnbroker, with his numerous family. Good, honest folk they were, who tried to make the house look fine, and the five daughters made the front stoop resplendent of summer evenings. But they had long ago moved up-town. Then it was a cheap boarding-house, and vulgar and flashy men and women swarmed out in the morning and in at eventide. Then it was a lodging [147] -house, and shabby people let themselves out and in at all hours of the day and night. And last of all it had become a tenement-house, and had fallen into line with its neighbors to left and right, and the window-panes were broken, and the curse of misery and poverty and utter degradation had fallen upon it.

But still it lifted its grand stone front, still it stood, broad and great, among all the houses in the street. And it was the old man's custom, after he had stood on the opposite sidewalk and gazed at it for a while, to go to a little French *café* a block to the eastward, and there to take a glass of *vermouth gommé*—it was a mild drink, and pleasing to an old man. Sometimes he chanced to find some one in this place who would listen to his talk about the old house—he was very grand; but they were decent people who went to that *café*, and perhaps would go back with him a block and look at it. We would not have talked to chance people in an east-side French *café*. But then we have never owned such a house, and lost it—and everything else. [148]

Late one hot summer afternoon young Rand sat in his studio, working enthusiastically on a "composition." A new school of art had invaded New York, and compositions were everything, for the moment, whether they composed anything or nothing. He heard a nervous rattling at his door-knob, and he opened the door. A young woman lifted a sweet, flushed, frightened face to his.

"Oh, John," she cried, "father hasn't come home yet, and it's five o'clock, and he left home at nine."

John Rand threw off his flannel jacket, and got into his coat.

"We'll find him; don't worry, dear," he said.

They found him within an hour. The great city, having no further use for the old Dolph house, was crowding it out of existence. With the crashing of falling bricks, and the creaking of the tackle that swung the great beams downward, the old house was crumbling into a gap between two high walls. Already you could see through to where the bright new bricks [149] were piled at the back to build the huge eight-story factory that was to take its place. But it was not to see this demolition that the crowd was gathered, filling the narrow street. It stood, dense, ugly, vulgar, stolidly intent, gazing at the windows of the house opposite—a poor tenement house.

As they went up the steps they met the young hospital surgeon, going back to his ambulance.

"You his folks?" he inquired. "Sorry to tell you so, but I can't do any good. Sunstroke, I suppose—may have been something else—but it's collapse now, and no mistake. You take charge, sir?" he finished, addressing Rand.

Jacob Dolph was lying on his back in the bare front room on the first floor. His daughter fell on her knees by his side, and made as though she would throw her arms around him; but, looking in his face, she saw death quietly coming upon him, and she only bent down and kissed him, while her tears wet his brow.

Meanwhile a tall Southerner, with hair halfway [150] down his neck, and kindly eyes that moved in unison with his broad gestures, was talking to Rand.

"I met the ol' gentleman in the French *café*, neah heah," he said, "and he was jus' honing to have me come up and see his house, seh—house he used to have. Well, I came right along, an' when we got here, sure 'nough, they's taihin' down that house. Neveh felt so bad in all my life, seh. He wasn't expectin' of it, and I 'lowed 'twuz his old home like, and he was right hahd hit, fo' a fact. He said to me, 'Good-day, seh,' sezee; 'good-day, seh,' he says to me, an' then he starts across [151] the street, an' first thing I know, he falls down flat on his face, seh. Saw that theah brick an' mortar comin' down, an' fell flat on his face. This hyeh pill-man 'lowed 'twuz sunstroke; but a Southern man like I am don't need to be told what a gentleman's feelings are when he sees his house a-torn down—no, seh. If you ever down oweh way, seh, I'd be right glad— —"

But Rand had lifted Edith from the floor, for her father would know her no more, and had passed out of this world, unconscious of all the squalor and ruin about him; and the poor girl was sobbing on his shoulder.

He was very tender with her, very sorry for her—but he had never known the walls that fell across the way; he was a young man, an artist, with a great future before him, and the world was young to him, and she was to be his wife.

Still, looking down, he saw that sweetly calm, listening look, that makes beautiful the faces of the dead, come over the face of Jacob Dolph, as though he, lying there, heard the hammers of the workmen breaking down his [152] father's house, brick by brick—and yet the sound could no longer jar upon his ear or grieve his gentle spirit.